THE CUPCAKE CONUNDRUM

A Williamsville Inn Story

BRIGHAM VAUGHN

Two Peninsulas Press

©Brigham Vaughn

Editing by Sally Hopkinson

Formatting by Brigham Vaughn

Cover design by Brigham Vaughn

Cover Images:

© DistanceO/Shutterstock

© rh2010/AdobeStock

© JJAVA/AdobeStock

Printed in the United States of America

First Printing 2020

AUTHOR'S NOTE

After Hank Edwards wrote the Christmas stories set in the Williamsville Inn Universe, I had no intention of writing another book in that world.

But when Hank mentioned he had an idea for one called *The Cupid Crawl*, Seth's brother Adrian grinned at me and said he'd like his story told too. I couldn't resist. When Ajay piped up and told me he was Seth's roommate and had been ghosted by Adrian, I was even more intrigued. That sounded like a challenge!

Writing about a character who had a far different cultural upbringing than I did was an even more daunting challenge though and at times I worried I wouldn't be able to do it justice.

Tesearch helped and so did connecting with a reader who patiently answered many of my questions and offered her own insight into what it would be like to grow up as a second generation Indian-American person trying to navigate a relationship with his parents. I hope I managed to do it honestly and respectfully. Many thanks to Mehjabeen Ashruff Siddiqui for her help with the research. Any mistakes made are my own.

Thank you to Hank Edwards who let me rejoin the Williamsville Inn world and offered valuable insight when I got stuck on the plot. Thanks to Helena Stone, Mehjabeen Ashruff Siddiqui, and Hank Edwards for another round of beta reading, and to Sally Hopkinson for her stellar editing work.

As always, a big thank you to all of you readers and fans who help make this possible. I couldn't do it without you.

I hope no matter what time of year you read this story, it will bring a little love and sweetness into your world!

I have a lot of new and exciting plans in the works after this, so if you'd liked to keep up with them, please sign up for my newsletter or join my reader group. Happy Reading!

JANUARY 2018 - MANHATTAN, NEW YORK

Adrian Cobb glanced around the bar. It was typical for a nice hotel, with a wooden counter, leather stools, and skilled bartenders. But the liquor selection was better than average and so was the appearance of the bartenders. Adrian had been looking. Not creepily, he hoped. But it had been a very long time since he'd been on the market, and it was nice just to enjoy the view and wonder what it would feel like to have that man's long, lean torso stretched out over his as they kissed or feel the brush of that woman's breasts as she slithered down his body.

It was a relief to be away from the bakery and the kids and all the pressures and responsibilities in his life. He was thirty years old and most days he felt a decade older than that. Seeing a woman curve her lips up in a smile at him as he ordered a drink or watch the muscles in a guy's forearms bunch as he shook liquor and ice together felt like an escape from Adrian's day-to-day life. A very, very welcome escape.

"Is this seat taken?"

Adrian glanced over to see a handsome guy smiling at him. He had warm brown skin, jet black hair, and his smile almost knocked Adrian off his bar stool. *Wow.*

"Uh, no. Have a seat," Adrian said, feeling a bit flustered and a lot dazzled. "Please."

The man had on a crisp blue shirt and a lanyard around his neck that indicated he was attending the same baking expo Adrian was. Not really a surprise since their group had taken over the entire hotel and conference center.

"I'm Adrian." He held out a hand. "Certified Master Baker."

The stranger coughed. "I'm sorry, did you say certified *masturbater?*"

"Master. Baker," Adrian enunciated. That joke was getting seriously old. He'd heard it at least a dozen times already today.

"Sorry, you're probably sick of that," the guy said with a little grin that did nice things to Adrian's stomach. "That's honestly what I heard at first, though. Or maybe that's just what I wanted to hear." He winked.

"Uhh." Adrian blinked at him, unsure how to respond.

"Wow. I'm really making an ass of myself, aren't I?" He smiled widely at Adrian as he shook his hand. "Let's start over. It's nice to meet you, Adrian. I'm Jay. Pastry chef."

"Nice to meet you, Jay the pastry chef."

"Can I buy you a drink?"

Adrian looked down at his nearly empty glass. "Uh, sure. Another whiskey sour would be nice."

Adrian studied Jay as he ordered drinks for both of them. He appeared to be a few inches shorter than Adrian, with broad shoulders and a lean body. His sleeves were rolled up to show off toned forearms, and he looked relaxed and at ease as he pulled out his wallet and smiled at the bartender. His thick black hair was swept off his forehead, and heavy stubble covered his jaw and framed his full lips. Wow. Jay was one of the best-looking guys Adrian had seen in a long time. And he'd sought Adrian out. The thought sent a little flutter of excitement through Adrian's stomach. Hell, yes.

Jay turned to him with a little smirk, and Adrian jerked in surprise, realizing he'd been caught staring. But Jay's gaze was bold, and that little smirk turned into something bigger.

"So, what's a handsome guy like yourself doing sitting all alone at the bar?"

Adrian shrugged. "Just killing some time. Debating if I'll go to one of the events tonight or not." Truthfully, he didn't know anyone else here, and while he wasn't afraid to chat up strangers, he always felt a little uncomfortable intruding on established groups. He'd turned down an invitation to go out to dinner with one of them. He figured he could always order room service if he got hungry later. "What about you?" Adrian countered.

"Same." Jay shrugged.

"Here you go, gentlemen." The bartender set their drinks in front of them.

"So, where are you based out of?" Jay asked after he turned back to face Adrian.

"Pittsburgh. You?"

"I'm here in New York. I'm head pastry chef at The Kensington. It's a 5-star boutique hotel in Brooklyn." The expression on Jay's face was a mixture of pride and embarrassment. "Ignore that. I sound like I'm bragging, don't I?"

"Hey, I led with my title, hoping to wow you. And head pastry chef at a place like that is impressive as hell." Especially since Jay was clearly not much older than Adrian. Mid-thirties at most.

Jay smiled. "Sometimes. What about you?"

"Oh, I own a small bakery. It's called King of Tarts."

Jay's dark brown eyes lit up. "Great name."

"Thanks. I was pretty pleased when I came up with it," he admitted with a small smile.

"How long have you been open?"

"Six years," Adrian said proudly. "The first few years were tough, but we're doing okay now." Not as well as he'd like, but he was getting there. When he got discouraged, he remembered that steady upward progress every year was something to celebrate. About fifty percent of small businesses failed within the first five years, so he was ahead of the curve.

"Do you like running your own business?"

Adrian sighed. "Sometimes. Sometimes, it's exhausting managing it all on my own. It's killed my social life. Not to mention my marriage. But I am proud of what I do."

Jay's gaze raked over him. "You're divorced then?"

"Yeah. Well, not officially. We're legally separated, not living together anymore. The papers have been filed, and we're just waiting for a court date."

"Amicable or no?"

Adrian's laugh was a little bitter. "No. I would have liked to keep it as civil as possible, but my ex was ..." He swirled his drink in his glass. "Not on board with that." He swallowed another sip of the cocktail, enjoying the pleasant burn as it went down.

"Sorry. Sore subject?"

"It's fine. We were both miserable, but I was the one who officially ended it, so I'm the bad guy." He glanced over at Jay. "What about you? Is being a pastry chef at a fancy hotel any easier on your romantic life? I'm guessing probably not based on what I know of the business."

"It can be tough," Jay said with a sigh. "I'm going through a dry patch at the moment, that's for sure. And in general, the hours I work ensure I'm single more than in relationships."

"No one is waiting for you to come home tonight then?"

"A couple of roommates but we're not involved. They're great guys but not my type."

"Not into men?" Jesus, Adrian was flirting. It had been so long he'd thought he'd forgotten how, but maybe he wasn't quite as rusty as he'd thought.

"I didn't say that." Jay's lips curled up in a little smile.

"Oh, yeah?" Adrian shifted a little to look at Jay more closely, and their knees brushed. Jay didn't pull away so neither did Adrian.

"Yeah. Out and proud gay man here."

"Out and proud but very, very rusty with men bi guy here." Adrian had to look away. His ears were hot and his heart was thumping so hard in his chest he was sure Jay could probably hear it.

"Rusty, huh?"

"It's been a long time." Adrian glanced at him out of the corner of his eye. "Like a decade and some change. Wait, no, my ex-wife and I tried a threesome with another guy a while back. I guess that was the last time."

"Didn't go well?"

"Depends on who you ask." Adrian's laugh was short and a little bitter. "I enjoyed myself and she was fine when we were focused on her, but she got very weirded out watching me with another man."

"What a shame."

"It was unpleasant, but I don't know, I don't think group stuff is really my thing, anyway. Not that I'm putting down people who are ... it's just ..." Adrian shook his head. "Never mind. I'll stop before I dig myself even further into this hole."

Jay smirked at him. "You're fine. I've done it occasionally. I can take it or leave it."

"Good to know." And that was even dumber sounding. Why was he so damn bad at this? Ugh. Rusty didn't begin to cover it.

Jay rested a hand on his thigh; it felt burning hot even through the denim. "What is your thing?"

Adrian had to consider the question for a moment. "I ... don't know. I guess I haven't thought about it in a while."

"Is that something you'd like to think about?" Jay leaned in a little but not enough to crowd him. "Because I'm thinking if you're interested, this might be the perfect opportunity. You're staying here in New York for the weekend ... I have nowhere I have to be either ..."

"I'm interested," Adrian said hoarsely. "I take it the feeling is, uh, mutual?"

"Yes." Jay rubbed a thumb across Adrian's thigh, sending little sparks through Adrian's body.

His skin was hot, and his head felt a little dizzy with desire as he tossed back the rest of his drink. "I have a room upstairs," Adrian offered.

Jay's smile widened. "Lead the way."

———

"Put your hands up against the wall," Jay said in his ear, his voice husky.

"Like this?" Adrian's heart beat a little faster as he pressed his palms to the tiles.

Jay covered his hands with his own and slid them into position, then coaxed Adrian into a wider stance. He gulped as Jay sunk to the floor of the bathtub. *Oh. Oh, hell.*

"I love how muscular your thighs are," Jay said, running wet hands across them.

"Yeah?" Adrian let out a shaky breath.

"Oh, yeah." Jay dragged his tongue across Adrian's left hamstring, then bit down. "So fucking sexy. And your ass ..." He made a noise of appreciation that went straight to Adrian's cock.

"But this is what I've been dying to see." He spread Adrian's cheeks wide. "Mmmm, yes. Perfect."

Adrian's cock pulsed. "Oh, shit," he whispered.

"And taste." Adrian could feel Jay's breath on his sensitive skin before he felt the swipe of a warm tongue.

Adrian rested his forehead against the slick tiles as Jay licked his ass. Combined with the steam from the hot shower, it made Adrian's head spin. And when Jay reached up and stroked his cock as he pushed his tongue deeper, Adrian almost lost it. He grabbed for Jay's hand and stilled him.

"I'm going to come if you keep that up."

"Okay." Jay pressed a kiss to his right cheek before he stood. His wet skin slid across Adrian's back as he pressed close, pushing Adrian up against the shower wall, his cock hard against Adrian's ass.

"Have you ever been fucked?" Jay whispered in his ear.

"A few times," Adrian managed. "It's just been ... a really long time."

Jay gripped his hips, dragging his cock along Adrian's crack. "You good with it as long as I take it slow?"

"Oh, yeah." He'd probably never wanted anything more in his life.

"Then let's get out of here."

Adrian's head spun as he groped for the faucet and turned off the tap. He felt half out of his mind as he hurriedly dried off and stumbled out of the bathroom. The air in the room was cold on his damp skin as he stood beside the bed, but he couldn't find it in himself to care. He was boiling on the inside.

"How do you want me?" he asked hoarsely.

Jay wrapped a hand around the back of his neck, then kissed him deeply. "Hands and knees," he whispered after he drew back. Adrian scrambled onto the bed as quickly as he could manage and got into position. He felt very exposed this way but despite the fact that they barely knew each other, he trusted Jay.

Adrian shivered as Jay explored his cleft with lube-slicked fingers, then dipped one inside his hole.

Jay was careful and he didn't rush, but he wasn't tentative as he fucked Adrian open with one, then two fingers. And when he slid three in, Adrian put his head down on the mattress and thrust his hips back. God, he'd missed that. That feeling of pressure and fullness.

"Ready for my cock?" Jay asked.

"Yeah," Adrian rasped.

He held his breath in anticipation as he heard the tear of foil from the small pile of condoms on the nightstand, and he felt almost dizzy when Jay finally pressed inside him, as deep as he could go. And once he urged Jay to move, Jay placed his hands around Adrian's hips, and all Adrian could do was brace himself against the mattress and cry out.

This was *exactly* what had been missing from his life.

———

"You awake?" Jay nuzzled against Adrian's back.

Adrian stretched. "I am now."

"How'd you sleep?"

"Like a man who's had half a dozen orgasms."

"It wasn't that many." Jay sounded amused as he pressed a kiss to Adrian's shoulder blade.

"I lost count."

"That's a good sign, right?"

"Very." Adrian flipped onto his back, dislodging Jay's grip, but once Adrian was still again, he wrapped him up tight. "I don't think I'm rusty anymore."

"You never seemed very rusty to me."

"Good."

"But we should probably keep going. Just to make sure."

Adrian let out a sleepy little chuckle. "Well, we wouldn't want to find out the hard way."

"Speaking of hard ..." Jay reached under the covers and stroked Adrian's cock. "You could hammer diamonds with that thing."

Adrian smiled. "I don't think that's actually a phrase."

"Maybe it should be."

"Maybe we should do something about it."

"I do have a few ideas."

"Do you?" Adrian asked.

"Yes. *Many.*"

"Guess I should leave you to it then."

"Guess you should."

"We really should get down to the expo."

"We should."

"I guess we *could* be a little late." Adrian kissed Jay's chest. "I mean, there is this very, very sexy collarbone here that I need to pay attention to." He dragged his tongue along the skin there, then gently bit down.

"A sexy collarbone, huh?"

"So sexy." Adrian licked a stripe across it. Jay shuddered under him. "It's making me want to fuck you."

"Please do." Never losing eye contact, Jay reached out and grabbed blindly for a condom and the bottle of lube. "I like the thought of walking around today, knowing you've been inside me."

"Mmm." Adrian let out a little groan. "If you don't stop talking like that, I'm going to come before I can."

"Then you better get me ready."

It didn't take a lot of prep before Adrian was balls deep inside Jay. He'd fucked him the night before, and he accommodated Adrian's cock easily now. But Adrian's head still swam as he drew back, gripping Jay's thigh as he drove in.

In the dim bedroom, everything else in his life faded away. No bakery, no ex-wife, no kids. Adrian could think of nothing but Jay. Nothing but Jay and the tight grip of his body and the sexy collarbone Adrian bit again, just because he could. There was only Jay's hands in his hair and his soft, breathless moans against Adrian's mouth.

Adrian's whole body tingled as his strokes slowed, becoming almost languid.

"You trying to drive me crazy?" Jay asked breathlessly. He shifted his hips, already propped up on a pillow, allowing Adrian to drive in deeper.

"No," Adrian said with a moan. "I'm trying to make it last. If I could, I'd fuck you like this all day."

"What about all night?"

"That's for you fucking me."

Jay slid his hands down, grabbing Adrian's hips, driving him even deeper. "Adrian ..." It was a plea and a breathless moan.

"How close are you?" It felt like every nerve in Adrian's body was lit up. Tingling.

"Almost there. Just keep fucking me, deep and slow." Jay guided his rhythm. "Just like that."

A few sweet strokes later and Jay threw his head back onto the pillow, the cords in his neck taut and defined as he cried out his pleasure. Adrian followed, shuddering against Jay's body as he came with his own hoarse shout. He collapsed on top of Jay, burying his head against Jay's neck. Adrian nuzzled in, loving the smell of Jay's skin.

They lay there, panting for a while, and Jay stroking his back with slow sweeps of his palm. After a while, he had to withdraw and toss the condom, but he returned to the shelter of Jay's arms.

"I want to do this forever," he muttered. He froze, realizing what he'd said, but Jay just pressed a kiss to his forehead.

"Me too."

ONE

FEBRUARY 2019 - BROOKLYN, NEW YORK

"I'm really fucking glad you don't own any more shit than this, Seth," Adrian groused as he lifted what felt like the millionth heavy box into the trailer and wedged it into the cramped space. His arms were beginning to feel like noodles. Overcooked noodles at that. "I like to work out but this is ridiculous."

"You didn't have to come help," Seth countered, pushing his hair off his forehead.

"Hey, it's not every day my brother moves in with his boyfriend."

"It's not." As Adrian turned away, he caught a glimpse of a soft smile flickering across Seth's face.

"You're really happy with Erik, huh?" Adrian asked as he pulled the U-Haul door shut. There. That was the last of it. Thank God, because the whole thing was packed to the top. He'd be lucky if he could fit a rolled-up newspaper inside, much less anything bigger.

Seth leaned against the trailer. "I really am."

"I'm happy for you, then." And he was. Although, sometimes seeing them together sent a little pang through Adrian's chest.

"You don't want it for yourself?"

"Ugh, I do but I think that ship has fucking sailed." Adrian sighed. "Who the hell has time to meet anyone, anyway?"

"I'd suggest getting snowed in at a hotel with a stranger. Worked for me!"

Seth had met Erik Josef at an airport a little over a year ago and wound up sharing a room at a hotel just outside of Buffalo, New York. They'd been a little cagey on some of the details of their first meeting, but Adrian had gotten the impression it was *not* love at first sight. Erik had been fresh off a divorce and hadn't even realized he was attracted to men. And Seth ... well, Adrian loved his brother but he could be a bit of a manwhore—or maybe that was just envy talking because fuck had it been a long time since Adrian got laid—so that had to have made for an interesting first meeting. Though clearly, it had worked. Hardly a re-creatable *or* reliable way to meet the love of one's life, unfortunately.

Adrian lifted his baseball cap off and scratched his head. "Not quite sure how to manage that. Besides, it's a hell of a lot more complicated for me with the kids."

"I know." Seth gave him a sympathetic smile.

"Maybe after they're grown and off to college." They were eight and six, and he'd gone this long. What was another decade or so? Oh God, that was a depressing thought.

"That's another twelve years. Can you really go that long?"

"I don't think I have much of a choice." Adrian loved Molly and Josh, but holy shit, being a single dad and raising two kids definitely cut into his social life. Most days, he didn't mind. He went to work, he did the dad thing, he passed out in bed, and it was enough. Still, the nights got lonely sometimes, and when the kids were at his ex-wife's house ...

"You shouldn't be lonely," Seth said, and for a second, Adrian wondered if he'd spoken the words aloud before he realized it was obvious to anyone with half a brain ... single, divorced guy who didn't have time to date? Of course, he was lonely.

"Were you lonely before you met Erik?" Adrian countered.

"Sometimes." Seth's serious expression melted into a grin. "At least, I was getting laid on the regular, though."

"How do you know I'm not?"

He snorted. "You've gotta be kidding me, dude. You have *never* gotten laid on the regular. Well, maybe when things were good with Michelle at first but ..."

"Ugh. I hate you a little bit right now."

"Because I'm right?" Seth jabbed him with his elbow. "It's because I'm right, isn't it?"

"Fuck you. But, yes."

"Has there been anyone since you split?"

"One guy last year." Adrian's mind flashed back to the hotel room. Of a man sinking his cock inside Adrian and making him moan—

"Based on the look on your face it was good too. Why just a one-time thing?"

"It wasn't. Well, it was a weekend. It didn't go beyond that with him, though."

"The question still stands. Even if he wasn't the kind of guy you wanted a relationship with, why didn't you make it a regular hook up?"

"For a dude who's related to me, you're weirdly concerned about my sex life."

Seth gave him a lopsided grin. "I just hate to see you miserable. You've had such a rough couple of years and you deserve a break. You should get out there and enjoy yourself!"

"I should. Maybe I would have if you hadn't made me come to New York and help you move all your shit. How does one guy who travels all the damn time own so much stuff?"

"He picks it up on his travels?" Seth's grin was cheeky.

"Which is the same excuse you gave me for why you didn't hire a moving company."

"I don't trust them not to ruin everything! A lot of it is one-of-a-kind. I can't just order a replacement for the rug I bought at a market in Marrakesh."

"That makes you sound like such a fucking pretentious hipster. Oh wait, you're a thirty-four-year-old travel writer living in Brooklyn with over three hundred thousand Instagram followers. You *are* a fucking pretentious hipster."

"I'm moving to Philly today, so fuck you. And you're a thirty-one-year-old bakery owner who needs to learn some social media marketing skills for his business, so fuck you twice."

Adrian ignored that jab. Seth was totally right about his lack of social media skills. But that didn't mean he was going to admit that to his brother. Adrian went with deflection instead. "Why didn't your fiancé help with the move, anyway? Too rich to lift boxes himself?"

Seth flipped him off. "No. He had an important meeting today in Philly, and this was the only week-long stretch I had this month where I wasn't going to be traveling and ..." Seth looked a little bashful. "Well, we just wanted to get all settled in together so we could start the rest of our lives together as soon as possible."

Adrian hooted. "Who'd have thought you were such a romantic? The man with a guy in every port."

"I didn't sleep around that much," Seth protested. "I just ... enjoyed my travels."

"And the men along the way."

"From time to time." Seth looked unashamed.

"And you don't mind being tied down to just Erik now?" Adrian had been curious about how Seth would make *that* adjustment.

"Nope. He doesn't make me feel tied down, for one, even though we are monogamous. He's my home port."

"Jesus, you're a sap." Adrian gave his brother a soft smile. "But I am happy for you."

"Thanks." Seth squeezed his arm. "I guess that's why I'm worried about you. You deserve to be happy too."

"Thanks. I do appreciate that. And look, maybe you're right." Maybe dating was completely out of the question but casual sex didn't necessarily have to be. Maybe he could find a friend with benefits. "Even if I don't have time to go out and find a relationship, I should at least find someone to suck my dick regularly."

The crude words had their desired effect and Seth shuddered. "I really didn't need that visual in my head. Thanks."

"Too late now!" Adrian did love needling his brother. But Seth always gave as good as he got. "This is what you get for being nosy about my sex life."

A delivery truck drove by, sending a gust of wind whipping across them. It fluttered the hem of Adrian's flannel and T-shirt, and he shivered when it teased at his bare skin underneath. He'd stripped off his hoodie earlier because he'd worked up a sweat hauling things down from Seth's 4th-floor walkup, but now, he was chilled. He slapped his brother on the arm. "What are we doing hanging out here in an alleyway, anyway? C'mon. Let's go inside."

As they rounded the corner of the building, Adrian glanced up at the sky. The clouds looked heavy and dark, and he crossed his fingers it wouldn't rain. The last thing he wanted to do was drive a huge trailer on unfamiliar, slick roads in heavy traffic. He fished in his pocket for his phone and brought up his weather app as he followed Seth to the building's front door. When Seth stopped abruptly, Adrian nearly ran into him.

"Hey, thought you'd forgotten about me," Seth teased. "Nice of you to finally show up to help, roomie."

"Sorry I'm late! I got held up on the train." The words were rushed and breathless but the accent was pure New York and, worst of all, familiar. The hair on Adrian's arms stood up on end as he lifted his head to look at the man he had been convinced he'd never see again.

All the blood drained from his face when he saw Ajay Sunagar standing in front of him.

Shit.

TWO

FEBRUARY 2019 - BROOKLYN, NEW YORK

"Jay?" Adrian said hoarsely.

"Adrian." The blood had drained from Jay's face, making his normally rich brown skin tone look almost chalky. But he was every bit as handsome as he'd been when Adrian had first seen him a little over a year ago.

"Wait, you two know each other?" Seth's voice jolted Adrian out of the daze he'd been immersed in.

"Yeah, you could say that," Jay snapped. His jaw was clenched and he'd gone completely stone-faced. The warm brown eyes Adrian had loved looking into as Jay fucked him sent an icy shiver down his back now. *Double shit.*

"What? How?" Seth asked.

"The baking expo!" Adrian blurted out. Seth blinked at his loud tone, and Adrian winced, then cleared his throat. "You remember that international baking expo I went to last year?"

"Here in New York? Yeah. I was mad because you said you were going to visit me while you were here but you punked out on me."

Adrian had punked out on him because he'd been in bed with Jay. He just hadn't mentioned that part to his brother. He'd never mentioned Jay at all until today.

"Yeah, you'll apparently never let me forget it either."

"Nope. But so ... what does that have to do with Jay?" Seth's puzzled expression smoothed out. "Oh, you met there, huh? Well, that makes sense. Cool. What a small world!"

"Yeah, sure is," Jay said with a scowl as he brushed past.

"Hey, you okay?" Seth asked, grabbing his arm. "Did the interview not go well?"

"No, it didn't." Jay frowned. "It was fine at first, but once they got to the part in my resume about working for The Kensington, the entire tone changed. I went through my whole spiel about the fact that I'd had nothing to do with the situation there, but I'm completely tainted by it. It's this *thing* hanging over my head that I can't get escape." Jay's shoulders slumped as he let out an exhausted-sounding sigh. "I just don't know what to do anymore."

Adrian frowned in confusion. Clearly, something had happened with Jay's position at The Kensington Hotel but he hardly felt like he was in a position to ask about it. Not after the way he'd fucked up last year. And, Jesus, if looks could kill, the one Jay had given him a few minutes ago could have leveled a three-block radius. He clearly wasn't over it.

"Hey," Seth's tone was soothing. "You did nothing wrong. And you've got three interviews lined up in Philly at really promising places this week. That's why you're coming with me, right?"

"I thought it was just for the heavy lifting," Jay's tone was joking but it sounded forced, and his smile was wan.

"Nah, that's why we've got him." Seth jerked his thumb at Adrian.

Adrian flexed, though with his flannel on, it was probably hard to see anything. And while Seth chuckled, Jay's scowl only deepened.

"Hope he's reliable," Jay said. There was a sneering note in his voice that made Adrian flinch, and Seth gave them both puzzled glances.

"He's my brother. Of course, he is. And—" A blaring horn cut him short.

"Hey, buddy, get your fucking truck out of the way! I need to get in that alley," a guy yelled from inside a utility van.

"Shit," Adrian muttered. They'd been lucky that there was an alley between the building Seth lived in and the one next door. It had been just wide enough for him to pull into, but they couldn't stay there forever. "Give me a minute and I will!" he called back.

"I don't have a fuckin' minute! I'm holding up traffic already."

Adrian groaned when he saw the cars lining up behind the utility van. Someone honked once, which kicked off a whole round of honking that set off a car alarm. "Well, go grab your shit, Seth. I've gotta get this moved. I'll circle around the block a time or two, pick you up, and take you to where Erik's car is parked," he shouted over the cacophony.

"Okay. C'mon." Seth tugged at Jay's arm. "We've gotta move. I hope you've got all your stuff together for the next few days."

"Yeah, I'm all packed. I just need to grab my charger and ..." Jay's voice trailed off as they strode toward the building. Adrian stared after them a moment, frowning. Wait, did that mean Jay was coming with them? Seth had mentioned earlier that his roommate was coming along to help with some of the lifting. And Adrian had figured out from the earlier conversation that Jay was going to Philly for job interviews, but he hadn't really had time to consider what that all meant. Oh, shit. This was going to be awkward as hell.

"Get your fucking ass in gear, man!" The guy in the van yelled, jolting Adrian into action.

"I'm going, I'm going," Adrian muttered as he jogged toward the alley. He'd deal with the situation with Jay later. For now, he had to move the truck and try not to piss off all of Brooklyn.

Backing up his truck with the trailer was no easy task, especially with the utility van impatiently waiting to pull into the alley where he'd been parked. Not to mention the irate drivers backed up behind that van, but eventually, Adrian got going in the right direction without hitting anyone or anything, and he made a slow loop around the block. In the process, he got flipped off by drivers he'd pissed off earlier at least three times, and by the time he pulled back up alongside Seth's building, he was ready to get the fuck out of the city. He liked New York but only long enough for short visits.

Thankfully, he spotted Seth and Jay on the sidewalk as he approached. Seth jogged up to his pickup, and Jay followed more slowly, glowering at him.

"We've got to hurry," Adrian said as he pushed the armrest and cup holder up to reveal the bench seat. "Just hop in now. We'll figure out the driving arrangements later."

A minute later, accompanied by the sound of blaring horns and expletives, Adrian pulled away from the curb. Somehow, Jay had ended up in the middle, and he was pressed against Adrian's side with an overnight bag on his lap. Seth carried a bag too and was on his other side.

"Sorry this is a little cozy," Adrian said apologetically. "It's a good size for a pickup but not great for three fully grown men." There was a second row of seats in the truck but they were packed with Seth's crap too.

"It's fine," Seth said. "You two will be comfortable enough once I leave."

"Wait, what?" Jay sounded horrified. "I thought I was riding with you, Seth?"

"No, you can't. Erik's car is already full. We loaded stuff up in there this morning and even the passenger seat is packed. I don't even want to think about how much work it would take to clear it out and put it here in the truck."

"Besides, I really need a clear view of both mirrors and the trailer behind me," Adrian said as he navigated toward the stupidly expensive parking lot where they'd stashed Erik's stupidly expensive car. "Or I'm going to end up in a wreck on I-95."

Adrian felt Jay's sigh as much as he heard it. He didn't blame Jay for not wanting to be trapped in the car with him for a few hours. Adrian wasn't exactly looking forward to the situation either.

"I'd offer to drive this but I don't feel comfortable handling a big-ass truck and a trailer when I've never driven either before. I'm definitely not about to do it for the first time between New York and Philly," Seth said, and Adrian nodded his agreement. The trailer had been rented in his name, and he really didn't want to get slapped with a bunch of fees if Seth fucked it up. Adrian trusted his brother, but he really didn't have that kind of money to burn. Everything he made went to the bakery or his kids. At least, since his ex-wife Michelle had a good job as a loan officer at a car dealership and she'd kept the house, he wasn't drowning in alimony payments. It was the only thing that kept him afloat at the moment.

"Could Jay drive Erik's car?" Adrian offered. "Then you could ride with me, Seth."

"I don't drive," Jay sounded resigned. "Native New Yorker here so I never learned."

"Right, you grew up in Queens," Adrian said and both Seth and Jay shot him a glance, one surprised he knew that and the other undoubtedly shocked he'd remembered. But Adrian hadn't forgotten a thing about Jay. Even if it had been nearly a year since they saw each other last.

"What's the big deal, anyway?" Seth said with a little laugh. "You two already know each other. You can use the drive to catch up. It'll be fine. It's only a couple of hours."

———

Unfortunately, what was supposed to be just over a two-hour drive quickly stalled out in the wake of an accident on I-95 due to rain. Slick roads had led to a four-car pileup. Adrian had put the truck in park twenty minutes ago, and he'd been staring at the ass-end of a semi-truck through sheets of pouring rain ever since. The radio was on, though low, and there had been no conversation to break up the monotony.

The rain could have made it feel cozy and intimate inside the truck cab, but Jay sat stone-faced and silent on the seat next to him. Once Seth had gotten out, Jay had crammed himself up against the door of Adrian's truck, put down the armrest, and piled his bag and coat up next to it, effectively creating a barrier between them. Despite the heater pumping out warm air, the atmosphere was decidedly frosty.

Adrian cleared his throat. "So, uh, I feel like I owe you an apology."

Jay sucked in a sharp breath. "You're kidding me, right?"

"No?" He hadn't meant for that to come out like a question. "No, I'm not kidding. I know I fucked up."

"Yeah, no shit." Jay's laugh was a little hollow. "I think that's putting it mildly."

"I am sorry. I shouldn't have let things end the way they did."

"You *ghosted* on me, Adrian!" Jay snarled.

"I ..." Adrian scrubbed a hand over his face, then glanced up at the semi ahead of them. Nope, they still weren't moving. "I didn't *mean to*."

"We had an incredible weekend together, talked about trying to make the distance thing work, I gave you my number, and I fucking never heard from you. How does that *accidentally* happen?"

"It wasn't accidental," Adrian admitted. "I made a choice. A *bad* choice, in hindsight, but ..."

"But *what*?"

"I have kids, okay!" he blurted out.

"Uh, okay?"

"Two kids. They're eight and six."

Jay recoiled. "That's why you disappeared on me? Because of your children?"

"I didn't know how you felt about kids! If you wanted them someday. If you would be okay being a stepdad eventually … I got all up in my head about it, and I got cold feet. It seemed crazy to try to make a long-distance thing work when I hadn't told you about my kids, and I … I panicked, okay? I ignored your messages and I figured you'd just move on."

"You asshole." Jay's voice was venomous. "You should have *asked*. If you'd bothered to be honest with me, I would have told you I *do* want kids. I just haven't found the right guy to get involved with. And dating someone who already has kids has never been a deal-breaker for me. A guy I was with a few years ago had a couple of teenagers, and I loved being a part of their lives. We broke up for entirely unrelated reasons—namely because he had to move out of state because his ex-wife got a great job else-where, and he didn't feel like he could ask me to give up my job at the hotel—but fuck you. Fuck you for assuming all of that without even asking how I felt."

"Shit." They stared at each other. "I really fucked up, Jay."

"Yeah, I guess you really did."

Adrian's stomach felt hollow as he stared at the truck ahead of him. Fucking up didn't begin to cover it.

Jay was silent for a few minutes. "You didn't lie about your marriage, did you?" he finally asked.

"What? No, I told you the truth! I was divorced at the time. Well, separated. The divorce hadn't been finalized yet. But we were legally separated like I told you. I swear I didn't cheat on anyone."

"Okay. So why the fuck didn't you tell me you had kids, then? I thought we basically covered everything, but apparently, you left out huge chunks of your life." Jay sounded bitter. "So that's a fun new thing to learn."

Adrian swallowed hard. "That weekend felt like ... like a fantasy. I was just enjoying being with you. Having a break from my daily life of being a dad. I left New York last year with every intention of calling you, but I got home and I was smacked in the face with the reminder that I've got two kids depending on me. I've got a bakery to run, you work an insane number of hours, and it suddenly seemed ludicrous that we could try to make a relationship happen when we live in different cities. In different states! And I rationalized it by saying you probably didn't want kids anyway, and even if you did, you probably didn't want to get saddled with someone else's kids and ..." Adrian closed his eyes. "I just figured it was easier for both of us if I made a clean break of things."

"A clean break?" Jay's laugh was hollow. "That wasn't clean. It was messy as hell. I spent weeks waiting for you to respond. Months wondering what I'd done wrong. If *anything* about our time together had been real. I beat myself up, thinking *I'd* fucked up somehow. So fuck you and your clean break, Adrian."

Jay fumbled for something in his bag and pulled out a pair of headphones. He jammed the plug into his phone and started to slide them over his ears, but Adrian grabbed his arm to stop him. "Wait, Jay ... let's talk more. I don't want to leave things this way."

"Well, I think I've heard quite enough from you at this point, and I really have nothing more to say." Jay settled the headphones on his head and looked out the passenger window.

Adrian let his head fall back against the headrest with a sigh. Damn it. That had gone far worse than he'd anticipated. At the time, he'd honestly believed—and maybe he'd just been trying to justify it in his head—that Jay would be disappointed for a very short while before he got over it. A minor let-down before he moved on. But clearly, Jay *hadn't* moved on. It brought a lump to Adrian's throat, thinking about Jay blaming himself and wondering what he'd done wrong. That wasn't what he'd intended at all. He'd liked Jay; honestly, genuinely liked him as a human being. Sure, the sex had been hot—scorching, in fact.

They'd spent most of the expo in Adrian's hotel room, engaged in the kind of raw, intense sex Adrian had assumed was something other people pretended actually existed. He'd certainly never experienced it before in his own life. But apparently, it did exist. That weekend, they'd spent every spare moment touching and tasting and exploring nearly every possible sexual activity that could happen between consenting adult men. Well, maybe not some of the more extreme kinks, but they'd discovered a few minor ones that Adrian had never dreamed of trying before.

And certainly hadn't tried since.

His face went hot at the memory of being pressed against the shower wall while Jay fingered him and stroked his cock. Jay had brought him to the edge, over and over, until he was a panting, begging mess. Adrian's blood heated just thinking about it now, and he had to shift in his seat as his cock started to harden.

But it had been a whole lot more than the sex. They'd both gone into it thinking it was a no-strings-attached fling, but by the end of the weekend, there had clearly been strings. And Adrian had made promises. Promises he hadn't kept. He'd meant every word of them at the time, but after he'd gotten home, reality had reared its ugly head and scared him shitless. But it still didn't excuse his behavior.

Jesus, what had he been thinking?

What he should have done was send Jay a message and let him know he'd changed his mind. That would have been the decent thing to do.

Adrian had never meant to make Jay think he'd used him for sex, and then discarded him, but he should have realized how it would seem on Jay's side. And the thought that Adrian had hurt Jay so deeply felt incredibly shitty. That wasn't the kind of guy Adrian was. Or at least, not the kind of guy he wanted to be.

There was no denying what he'd done.

Adrian glanced over at Jay. His head rested against the passenger window and his eyes were closed. His lashes were thick and dark against his cheeks, and he breathed slowly and evenly. Adrian didn't think he was asleep though. There was too much tension in his jaw and shoulders. Adrian had seen Jay truly relaxed and content. He'd felt Jay's soft breath against his chest, felt Jay's arm, heavy with muscle and sleep, draped over his midsection. He'd woken Jay up with kisses and fallen asleep with the taste of him on his lips.

And now ... here they were.

The blare of a horn once again jolted Adrian to attention, and he glanced forward to see traffic moving. He eased the truck into drive and crept forward. When he glanced over, Jay's eyes were open and he stared at Adrian with an inscrutable expression. But traffic picked up after that, and by the time Adrian glanced over again, Jay's eyes were closed.

They didn't speak again until they reached Philadelphia.

THREE

As they approached the outskirts of the City of Brotherly Love, Adrian tapped Jay's thigh. "Hey, Jay? Do you have the address? I want to put it in my GPS." Jay's eyes flew open and he blinked at Adrian, clearly startled.

"What?" Jay pulled his headphones off, and Adrian realized he hadn't heard a thing he'd said.

"Do you have Seth and Erik's address handy? I know I have it somewhere, but I can't really look while I'm driving and there's nowhere to pull over."

Jay glanced around. "Where are we exactly?" His voice sounded a little hoarse and scratchy. Adrian wondered if he had actually fallen asleep.

"On the outskirts of Philly."

"Oh." Jay rubbed the back of his hand across his eyes. "Yeah, give me a second to get my brain in gear and I'll find the address. Seth sent it to me the other day, and it shouldn't be hard to find. I'll text it to you."

"Thanks." Adrian hesitated. "Actually, can you put it in here …" Adrian handed his unlocked phone to Jay. "I don't want to take my eyes off the road."

Jay let out an annoyed sounding huff but he did as Adrian asked. The vehicle was silent except for the GPS directing him to the loft in the Avenue of the Arts District. It occurred to Adrian that Jay hadn't had to ask for his number. He'd still had it in his phone. Had some part of Jay still been hoping to hear from him again? Or had he simply forgotten it was in there? But, no, that didn't make sense. He'd clearly remembered it was still in his phone. The thought did funny things to Adrian's stomach, but he wasn't sure how to ask the question without making the situation worse.

As they got close to the loft, Jay spoke. "I texted Erik. He said to go around the back of the building. There's a loading dock and a freight elevator we can use."

"Oh, thank fuck," Adrian said. "Hauling boxes down four flights of stairs was bad enough. I wasn't looking forward to carrying them up five."

Jay didn't answer.

Adrian found the building, then circled around to the back. As promised, there was a place where he could easily pull up, and he breathed a sigh of relief once the truck was parked. What should have been just over a two-hour drive had taken almost three and a half, and he was looking forward to stretching his legs.

Jay got out of the truck immediately, as if he couldn't wait to get away from Adrian.

Moving more slowly, Adrian sighed and caught a glimpse of himself in the rearview mirror as he reached for the door handle.

He looked tired. There were circles under his blueish-green eyes, and he paused to comb through his disheveled light brown hair with his fingers, hoping to pull himself together. Pointless, since Jay clearly didn't give a shit.

Adrian stepped out of the truck just as Seth pulled up beside him.

"Well, that took fucking forever," Seth grumbled when he got out of Erik's sleek Lexus.

"Tell me about it." Adrian stretched, feeling stiff as he twisted from side to side. His lower back popped, and for a moment, he wasn't sure if it was good or if he'd done something very, very wrong. The relief that spread through him a moment later answered that question. He could spend all day on his feet, making bread, rolling out cookies, and decorating cupcakes but sitting for more than three hours had nearly done him in.

"Hey there."

They both turned to see Erik striding toward them. His red hair shone in the early evening light, and he was dressed well as always, though how the man managed to make jeans and a simple pullover look like a million dollars, Adrian would never know. Jesus, his brother *did* have good taste in men. Adrian would take Jay any day of the week, though. He glanced over at him with a pang of regret. Damn it, he'd really fucked up big time, hadn't he?

"Glad you made it safely." Erik pulled Seth into an embrace and kissed him. When it clearly became more than a quick peck on the lips, Adrian looked away.

Unfortunately, his gaze landed on Jay again, who scowled at him.

The heat between Seth and his fiancé was palpable. It had been from the moment Seth brought Erik home to their parents' house over a year ago. Seth told their mother he was bringing a friend, but from the moment Adrian saw them together, it was obvious that it was far more than that. Adrian was happy for his brother, but way more than a little envious, he admitted to himself as they finally pulled apart.

"Hey, congratulations again on the engagement, by the way," Adrian said, holding out a hand to Erik. "I'm really happy for you both."

"Thanks." Erik gave him a genuine smile. He'd seemed a little serious at first, but the more Adrian got to know him, the more he liked him. He was certainly good for Seth. Few guys could tolerate Seth's erratic schedule as a travel writer, and Adrian knew Erik traveled a fair amount too. Adrian couldn't handle that kind of distance in his relationships—which was why a long-distance relationship with Jay had seemed like such a bad idea once he'd gotten home—but it seemed to work perfectly for Seth and Erik.

"Yeah, congratulations," Jay said. His tone was warm, and Adrian was startled to realize it was the first time he had really sounded like himself all day. "I'm a little pissed you're stealing my roommate, but otherwise, I'm happy for you guys."

Seth chuckled. "I feel pretty lucky to be moving in with this guy." He lightly bumped shoulders with Erik. "But I am sorry to lose you as a roommate. If you get a job in Philly, though, you'll be close enough that we can still hang out."

"No luck on the job front in New York, then?" Erik said.

"Not so far."

"What happened exactly?" Adrian blurted out. "Last year, it sounded like you loved the position at The Kensington."

Jay glanced over at him and scowled. "Yeah, well, that was last year. A lot has changed for me since then. I learned to stop trusting people."

Ouch.

Even the industrial ovens in Adrian's bakery had never burned him that badly.

Seth gave Jay a sympathetic look. "Look, the executive chef you worked for was an asshole but—"

"Can we not talk about that whole situation?" Jay said with a sigh. "I'm exhausted just thinking about it."

"Uh, sure." Seth looked surprised. "Moving on. When are your interviews?"

"I have two tomorrow and another one two days later."

"Awesome. I'm sure one of them will work out. And hopefully, you'll have two offers so you can get them both vying over you."

"I'd be more than happy with one."

"Let's cross our fingers for that then," Seth said cheerfully.

"Come on, let me take you upstairs and show you around," Erik said. "I'm sure you could use a short break before we get started moving Seth in."

Erik and Seth's loft was stunning. Adrian wasn't too big on architecture or design but even he could tell the place was impressive. The large foyer led into a huge open concept living, dining, kitchen area. It was a little stark and sparsely furnished, but once Seth's belongings had been moved in, it would be amazing.

"There's a half bath there," Erik said as he pointed to the left, just inside the door. "And a full bath there to the right, through the spare bedroom. Seth, you know where the one in the bedroom is.”

They dispersed quickly and Adrian took the one in the guest room when Jay made a beeline for the other.

When they reconvened in the spacious living room, Erik cleared his throat. “So, I’m not sure what we’re going to do for sleeping arrangements, exactly. It’s a two-bedroom place, plus a den. I didn’t really anticipate having this many guests at once when I bought the place,” Erik said, his tone apologetic. “I was single at the time and didn’t have any family besides my daughter, Joanna.”

“It’s fine.” Jay waved off the apology. “I appreciate you letting me crash here while I job hunt. We’ll figure it out.”

“Of course.” Seth smiled at him. “It’s the least we could do for your help with moving. And dealing with a new roommate.”

“Yeah, the new person seemed nice when I met them. And who knows? Maybe I’ll get a position here, and I’ll be moving out too.” Jay’s smile looked forced.

“We should probably get your stuff unloaded before we worry about sleeping arrangements,” Adrian said. He glanced at his phone to check the time. “We’ve only got a couple of hours to get it hauled up here, then get the trailer to the rental place.”

Seth let out a little groan. “Damn it, you’re right. Okay. Let’s go.”

With four people doing the heavy lifting, it actually didn’t take as long as Adrian had anticipated to unload the trailer and move the contents up to the apartment. He could have kissed the elevator in gratitude. They stashed Seth’s belongings in Erik’s den, but it was packed to the brim by the time they were done.

Erik surveyed it with a skeptical look. "How did you *fit* all of that in your place? You shared your apartment with three other people!"

"I had a storage unit in the basement," Seth admitted with a sheepish grin.

Erik pulled him in with one arm and kissed his temple. "Good thing my place is spacious and needed some life breathed into it, then."

"Good thing." Seth slid an arm around his waist and gave him an adoring look. They were almost sickening, and yet, Adrian had never been so envious of anyone in his life.

"Well, I should get going," Adrian said with a tight smile. "Gotta get the trailer returned or I'll have to pay for another day of use."

"Jay, why don't you go with Adrian to drop off the trailer?" Seth suggested. "He might need some help with navigation or something." His tone was casual but it looked like he was trying to communicate something with the pointed look he gave Jay, who opened his mouth like he was going to argue, then closed it with a sigh.

Oh. The pieces clicked into place for Adrian too. His brother wanted some alone time with his boyfriend. Adrian had no desire to be there for *that* reunion. And Jay probably didn't want to be either.

"Sure, you can help me navigate," Adrian said with a smile Jay didn't return.

"Let's get going," was all he said.

They walked in silence down to the truck, and Jay once again plastered himself to the passenger door.

"Good call on coming with me. Neither of us wanted to be in that apartment while they reconnect," Adrian said as he buckled his seatbelt. "It's been almost two weeks since they've seen each other and ..."

"Yeah, I'd rather have my fingernails pulled off one by one."

"Guess that makes me the lesser of two evils," Adrian joked. He pulled out his phone and did a quick search for the location. It was at least half an hour drive from where they were, which meant Erik and Seth would have more than an hour alone.

Jay shot him a look. "I wouldn't say *that*. In fact, I seriously thought about finding a coffee shop or a bar nearby to wait it out, but I didn't want to explain to your brother why I can't stand to be in the same room as you."

Ouch. The hits just kept coming.

"He has no idea what happened between us last year, then?" Adrian asked, trying to sound casual.

"No. I never told him."

"I'm surprised."

"We weren't living together at the time, and I had no idea you two were related. Seth and I've known each other for years, but I only moved in with him about six months ago. My lease came up right at the same time one of his roommates left. It seemed like the perfect solution for us both."

"How did you two meet in the first place?"

"Several years ago, he did a feature on the hotel restaurant. I helped him with the food styling for the photo shoot. The executive chef was too busy to be bothered." The disdain in Jay's voice was evident, and Adrian was dying to ask what had happened but he didn't want to push his luck. Jay was talking to him, and he didn't want to risk pissing him off again. "Seth sent me an email with a link to the article once it went live, and we started talking after that. When I found out he was looking for a roommate at the same time I was searching for a place, it seemed like an obvious fit."

"What are the odds?" Adrian said. "I mean that we'd meet, and then six months later you'd move in with my brother."

"Life's funny that way." But there was nothing amused in Jay's tone, and he lapsed back into silence.

———

Thankfully, Seth and Erik were both fully dressed by the time Adrian and Jay returned to the apartment. There was a suspicious glow to them both, and Seth's hair was still damp from a shower.

"I'm sure you're both starved," Erik said with a smile. "Dinner should be ready in about fifteen minutes if that works for you. If not, we can keep it warm for a while."

"That sounds good to me," Adrian said. He hadn't eaten since before he arrived at Seth's place earlier today, and his stomach rumbled at the good smells coming from the oven. Apparently, they'd had time to cook in addition to whatever else they'd gotten up to. That or Erik had planned ahead. Probably the latter.

"Sure." Jay nodded tightly. Seth and Erik exchanged a look that spoke volumes.

Clearly, they could tell that something was off with Jay. He was still very quiet as they ate, but Adrian asked about the upcoming wedding and Erik filled the silence.

"The renovations of the Williamsville Inn should be done in a few months, and we thought we'd hold the wedding there at the end of the summer. The place obviously holds special meaning to us, and well, that was one of the amenities we thought we'd focus on for the re-branding."

Adrian looked at Seth in surprise. "You're helping with the marketing?"

Seth shrugged. "Not officially. Holding events there was something Erik thought of long before we started talking about it. But there's a gorgeous courtyard, and the place has already been in the news because of the Rex Garland song, so we figured we could tie it all together."

"Oh, that's right," Adrian said. "He wrote that Christmas song there, didn't he?"

"And met the love of his life too," Erik said with a little smile at Seth.

The story about Rex Garland had been all over the news last year. The very famous and very gay singer had met a completely ordinary guy named Will, who was staying at the Williamsville Inn for work. Will had secretly helped the singer with the lyrics for his new song, and they'd fallen in love in the process.

When he'd read about it, Adrian had wondered what the hell had been in the water at that inn. And if he could get a little of it for himself.

"Erik says that like he had a clue who Rex Garland was when I mentioned him." Seth snorted. "We were sitting near them at the airport bar and he had *no* idea. He'd never even heard of him."

"I like his music now," Erik protested. "That has to count for something."

Seth just shook his head fondly. "Anyway, the inn has been getting some great press since then, but they haven't really expanded into events yet. We figured we'd kick off the marketing for that with our wedding and kill two birds with one stone. There's a whole marketing firm Erik's company works with, but they seemed very on board with leveraging my social media presence as well."

"What the hell, Seth? You've never offered to pimp out my bakery," Adrian scoffed. "Not a single photo of a loaf of bread or a cookie on your Instagram."

Seth's eyes gleamed. "Bake me some cupcakes while you're here, and I'll pimp you out all you want."

Adrian narrowed his eyes at Seth. "This is just a ploy to get me to make cupcakes for you, isn't it?"

"Yes. But my offer still stands."

Erik shook his head and glanced over at Jay. "Do you have siblings? I don't, so I'm never sure what to make of these two."

"Yeah, I have two older sisters, but we're not that close," Jay said quietly. "Big age gap."

And just like that, Adrian was back in a hotel bed with Jay.

"What's your family like?" Adrian asked. They were stretched out on the bed, sweaty and covered in various bodily fluids but too tired to move.

"You just fucked my brains out and you want to talk about our families?" Jay stretched an arm out and snagged a bottle of water off the nightstand.

"I've never really had sex with a stranger before," Adrian admitted. "I don't really know the protocol. Is getting to know the other person not allowed?" Truthfully, family was the first thing that had popped into Adrian's head when he was trying to figure out how to make conversation but he could admit it was probably a little weird.

Jay gulped down the water, his throat working noisily. Adrian watched, unable to tear his gaze away. He was definitely going to need to see Jay do that later. With something a hell of a lot more personal than a bottle of water.

"Depends on the people, I guess. I don't mind. I'm just not used to it. As far as my family? Well, my parents both came to the US from Bangalore, India as kids and met in college. My dad's a dentist, and my mom works in his office. I have two sisters, both older. Quite a bit older, actually. I was, uh, a surprise to everyone."

"Are you all close?"

"It's complicated. Most of my life, it was just my parents and me on a daily basis. My sisters ... well, we get along, but we don't have a lot in common. You?"

"Two brothers and a sister. I'm the youngest too, although, I never really feel like it. I got married young, so since then, I've felt more grown-up than my one brother. He travels a lot for work so he never really settled down. I'm not finding fault—he's amazing at what he does—he's just never had the kind of responsibilities I've had, you know?"

"Are you're close to your siblings?"

"Oh, yeah, we're all really close, actually. Except for my one brother—the world traveler—we're all in Pittsburgh. My parents still live there too. They've all been hugely helpful since the divorce. Running—" he bit off what he'd been about to say. His mom even got his kids off to school every morning he was at the bakery. He was there to tuck them in every night, though. Except when they were at Michelle's place. But there was no point in bringing all that up, right? Adrian wasn't a dad this weekend. Just some guy enjoying his time off. "Running errands for me if I need them, that sort of thing. They've been amazing."

"You said you were openly bi. I take it your family knows?"

"Oh, yeah. Plus, my one brother is gay so ..."

"How'd your parents take that?"

Adrian shrugged. "They were fine. When he came out, I threw in the 'oh, by the way, I'm bi' thing at the same time, and they just rolled with it all. My mom started suggesting I go out with 'that nice boy of Sharon's' and 'the cute girl at the grocery store'."

"That's sweet."

Adrian laughed. "Her meddling was a little obnoxious, but yeah, I know I'm lucky. How'd your parents' do when you came out?"

Jay dragged a hand over his face. "It was a little rough. Being gay was still illegal in India until 2017."

Adrian winced.

"How much do you know about Indian culture?"

He shrugged. "Not a ton. I went to school with a few Indian kids but …"

Jay nodded. "Well, like I said earlier, it's … complicated. My parents came here in the 70s. There wasn't a huge Indian community here then, so a lot of the immigrants were nervous about the new customs and afraid their kids would get corrupted by their American friends and forget their Indian heritage completely." Jay rubbed at his face again. "My grandfather worked for an import/export business in Bangalore, so he had a lot of dealings with Americans. It was a little less of a culture shock for my parents than for some, but they were still very concerned about us becoming too westernized."

Adrian nodded. "That can't have been easy for them as parents. Or for you and your sisters."

"Yeah, it was tough. I straddled this weird line of being too brown and Indian for white people and too white and American for the Desi community."

"I've heard that term but I don't really know what it means," Adrian admitted.

"Desi? Uh, well the people and culture that come from the Indian subcontinent; India, Pakistan, and Bangladesh are all lumped in together under the Desi umbrella."

"Okay." Adrian thought about what Jay had said. "I get that not feeling like you belong, although on a way smaller scale. As a bi guy, I'm too straight for gay people and too gay for straight people. I never quite feel like I fit anywhere."

Jay looked vaguely surprised. "Yeah, I hadn't thought of that."

"So your family wasn't okay with you being gay?"

"Not at first. We fought a lot. In the Hindu faith, the son is the one who lights his father's pyre at his cremation. They were concerned that my being gay would make that unacceptable. The fact that I'm their only son created more pressure."

"I can understand why that would be hard for them."

"It was difficult to work through, but now, they seem resigned to the idea. I know they'd be happier if I walked into their house and said that I was marrying a woman. They've met a few guys I've dated, and they've always been polite, but it's clear it's disappointing to them."

"That must be difficult."

"It can be sometimes." Jay offered him a wan smile. "The pastry chef thing wasn't great either. There was a lot of hand wringing and praying to Krishna for a while. They were concerned that it wouldn't be a stable career. They got more comfortable with it, eventually, and I know my dad is really proud of me. He'll drop it into a conversation at the most random times too. Someone will ask what kind of bags he wants at the grocery checkout, and he'll say 'I brought my own. Oh, did you know my son is a pastry chef at The Kensington Hotel?' It's a little embarrassing, to be honest, but ..."

Adrian smiled. "It's sweet."

"Yeah. He does better with my career, and my mom does better with me being gay, so I guess it evens out a little. I know they'd both be happier about me being gay if I had a husband. We just don't talk about it much."

"At least, you're not getting set up by your mother."

"She might try if she knew any gay men. None of the Indian dating sites she knows about are queer-friendly, thankfully."

Adrian chuckled. "Meddling moms are totally universal, I think."

"Exactly." They shared a smile.

"So can I ask? Is Jay your given name or a nickname?"

"My given name is Ajay."

"Uh-jay?" Adrian repeated.

"Pretty close. It's spelled with an A, though. It was just easier to go by Jay in school, and I got used to the nickname. My parents are really the only people who call me Ajay."

Adrian nodded. "So, have you ever been to India?"

"Once, as a kid. I honestly don't remember that much about it. I know we went to visit some relatives near Bangalore. We went during the wet season —because I was on break from school—and it rained a lot. Other than that, I mostly remember being bored looking at the old temple ruins on the outskirts of the city. I just wanted to be back home with my friends."

"Yeah, at least, I had built-in friends with my brothers around," Adrian said.

They lapsed into silence.

"All right, I think that's enough talk about our personal lives," Jay said. "What do you say we get in the shower, clean up, then figure out something for dinner?"

"Sure. Are you thinking about going out to eat?" Adrian stretched.

Jay's gaze raked over Adrian's body. "No."

Adrian felt a shiver go through him at the promise in Jay's eyes.

"What the hell is up with you two?" Seth's exasperated tone broke through the fog of Adrian's memory. "Jay, you've been in a foul mood all day, and Adrian's on another planet."

"Just thinking about everything I should get done," Adrian lied.

"You are terrible at taking a vacation!"

He glanced over at Jay. "Tell me about it."

Look how badly it had gone the last time he'd done it.

FOUR

After dinner, they hung out in the living room, talking for a while, but it had been a long day for all of them, and Adrian wasn't sorry when Erik brought up the topic of sleeping arrangements again after Adrian yawned.

"So, like I said earlier, I'm afraid I—we—only have the one guest room," Erik explained. "We do have a very comfortable air mattress, though. We can set that up in the guest room if you don't mind sharing—"

"I do," Jay said, his words clipped.

Seth shot him a glance out of the corner of his eye. "We can set it up here in the living room then, I guess? The den is obviously way too full of boxes to squeeze a bed in."

"That's fine. I'll take the air mattress. Adrian can have the guest room."

"You sure you don't mind sleeping in the living room, Jay?" Seth asked.

"It's fine."

It clearly was not fine, and from the looks Seth and Erik gave Adrian, everyone knew it. *Fuck. This is getting monumentally awkward.* And from the pointed looks Seth kept giving both of them, he was going to interrogate whomever he got alone first.

"Well." Erik cleared his throat. "Guess we'll get that all set up now for you guys."

Erik and Jay set up the mattress while Seth showed Adrian around the guest room. "Towels are in there." Seth pointed to a shelf in the attached bathroom. I'm afraid you and Jay will have to share the bathroom." He lowered his voice. "What is going on with you two, anyway? You're both acting weird."

"Can we talk about this tomorrow?" Adrian asked quietly. He dragged a hand through his hair. He was exhausted and he just didn't have the energy to deal with it tonight. Especially when Jay could overhear.

"Yeah, of course." Seth shot him a concerned look. "You can tell me anything, though. You know that, right?"

"I do know." Adrian reached out and squeezed his shoulder. "I'm just fucking exhausted."

"Yeah, of course." Seth's expression smoothed out. "Don't hesitate to knock on our door if you need anything, okay?"

"I think I remembered to pack everything I need, but if something comes up, I'll let you know."

"G'night."

"Night, Seth."

After Seth disappeared, Adrian rummaged through his bag, looking for pajamas and his toiletry kit. He was looking forward to taking a hot shower, crawling into bed, and crashing hard.

As he pulled out his pants, he heard a soft, tentative knock on the door. He glanced up to see Jay in the doorway, an uncomfortable expression on his face.

"Mind if I use the shower?" Jay asked stiffly. He had a hanger with dress clothes dangling from his index finger. "I'm kinda sweaty from hauling boxes, and I want to make sure I get the wrinkles out of these clothes for my interview tomorrow."

"Uh, sure." Adrian tried to hide his annoyance. "Go for it."

Jay disappeared into the bathroom, pulling the door firmly closed behind him, which annoyed Adrian even further. Did he think Adrian was going to try to join him? No, Jay had made it abundantly clear that he wanted nothing more to do with Adrian.

He tossed his bag on the floor with a scowl and settled on the bed with his phone. He'd video chatted with the kids for a few minutes earlier tonight before dinner just to check in but they were perfectly happy to spend a little extra time at their mother's. He and Michelle had split custody 50/50 in court but neither minded being flexible about adjusting their schedules as necessary. They'd made a lot of mistakes in their marriage, but the one thing they'd done well was doing what was best for the kids. Adrian was grateful. Both their families helped out too, so in that regard, the kids probably had it way better than most. Seth's travel schedule and distance from Pittsburgh made it difficult for him to be as involved in person, but he liked to video chat with the kids and often sent the pictures and videos from his travels. Plus, he brought home the *coolest* gifts, according to Molly and Josh.

Adrian thought about all of the things Seth did to stay close to his niece and nephew and realized he was a monumental idiot. He could have done the same to stay in contact with Jay. They could have made it work if he'd given it half a chance.

Annoyed with himself, he checked some Penn State basketball scores, read a few news articles, then ran out of things to occupy his time. He was used to being at home with his laptop where he could crunch numbers for the business. There was always something to do, so even when the kids weren't home, he never felt like he had a shortage of work to occupy him. But now, all he could do was sit on the bed and think about the fact that the man in the shower a few feet away hated his guts.

Adrian sighed and rested his head against the wall, his thoughts drawn to memories of the weekend in New York.

He was so lost in those memories it wasn't until he heard the sound of water shutting off that he returned to reality and noticed he was hard. He reached down and squeezed his cock, feeling it pulse in his hand. When it was clear his erection wasn't going away any time soon, he shifted, crossing his legs and pulling his hoodie lower so his dick wasn't as visible, at least.

A few minutes later, Jay came out of the bathroom in soft-looking gray sweats and a dark green long-sleeve T-shirt. His wet hair was slicked back from his forehead, and he barely spared Adrian a glance. "Thanks."

"Sure. Of course. You heading to bed?"

"Yeah. Early interview tomorrow."

"Feel free to come in whenever you need to get ready in the morning."

"Thanks." Jay hesitated as if he were about to say something, then shook his head and walked toward the door. He left without another word, pulling the door shut behind him. When he was gone, Adrian let his head fall back against the headboard with a thump. Ugh. Well, that was all going about as well as he'd expected. On the plus side, the cold shoulder had worked as well as a bucket of ice water on his hard-on.

When Adrian went in the bathroom a short while later, he found Jay's dress clothes hanging on the hook behind the door. Adrian left them where they were. The scent of Jay's body wash still filled the air as Adrian showered. His thoughts kept drifting back to their weekend together, and after washing off the sweat and scrubbing his hair, he reached down and grabbed his dick. He was half-hard again, and he closed his eyes as he stroked, mentally replacing his own hand with Jay's.

Adrian reached around, slipping a finger inside himself. The water wasn't really enough to slick his entrance but he pushed deeper anyway, imagining it was Jay's finger, and a few strokes of his cock later, he came with a muffled shout.

He rinsed off, knowing there was probably something very sick and wrong about masturbating to thoughts of a man whose heart he'd broken. Guilt chewed at him as he got out of the shower and dressed. It lingered as he brushed his teeth and took out his contacts. Even as he settled into bed and turned out the light, it dogged him.

Adrian was the one who'd fucked up. He shouldn't be mad at Jay for being cold to him.

He'd gotten what he deserved.

———

Adrian awoke some time later to a muffled crash. It had come from outside the bedroom, and he clicked on the light beside the bed, blinking sleepily. When he heard a small groan from the hall, he quickly got out of bed. As he opened the door, the last thing he expected to see was a man lying on the ground with the air mattress half on top of him. Jay, presumably, but it was hard to tell.

"What the fuck?" Adrian whispered as he lifted the mattress, then propped it against the wall. "What the hell just happened?"

"I couldn't sleep. There is so much ambient city light in that living room I could fucking read by it. I figured I'd move my bed to the hallway here where it's a little darker, but I tripped over the rug and ..." Jay rubbed his knee. "Not one of my more graceful moments."

"Do you want to just sleep in the guest room with me?"

Jay stared open-mouthed at him for a moment. "Are you fucking serious? You treated me like shit last year and now you want to hook up again?"

"I didn't mean sleep together!" Adrian's voice rose, and Jay made a slashing motion with his hand. "Sorry. I was suggesting you drag the air mattress into the guest room," he said more quietly.

"Oh." Jay seemed to consider the idea. "Is it dark in there?"

"There're heavy shades. It's practically pitch black."

"Fine." Jay grasped one end of the air mattress, and Adrian automatically took the other. "It appears you're the lesser of two evils for a second time tonight."

"That's not exactly a ringing endorsement."

"It's not meant to be."

Adrian stifled a sigh and helped Jay maneuver the mattress into the room. He set it up as far as possible from the bed where Adrian slept. "We could trade if you want?" Adrian offered. "You could have the real mattress. I'm sure you want to be well-rested for your interview tomorrow."

"I'm fine." Jay disappeared through the door, and Adrian took a seat on the bed while he waited for him to return. A few minutes later, Jay appeared with an armful of blankets, a pillow, his phone, and a charger. Adrian got comfortable in bed again while Jay set up everything to his liking.

He slid under the covers, then pulled them up to his chest. "I'm all set. You can turn out the light."

"Okay." Adrian clicked off the lamp, plunging the room into darkness. There was the rustle of covers as they got comfortable, then silence except for their slow, even breathing.

"Thanks," Jay said gruffly.

Adrian had nearly been asleep again, and he jerked in surprise. "What?"

"For letting me sleep in here. This is much better."

"Oh. Good. Um, you're welcome. I'm glad I could help. It's probably the least I can do, right?"

Jay's silence was answer enough.

Adrian flipped onto his side as guilt settled into the pit of his stomach once more. That wasn't going to go away any time soon.

Every moment from the weekend they'd spent together continued to taunt him. The good and the bad. His thoughts drifted back to their last day at the expo.

"This weekend has been amazing."

"It has." Jay kissed him. "I know we said at the beginning that this was just a hookup but …"

Adrian ran a hand across Jay's chest, feeling the smoothness of his skin. "But it doesn't feel like it, does it?"

"No."

"It would be crazy trying to make something long distance work. With the hours we both work and …" and my kids, he finished in his head. He still hadn't told Jay about them. God, if there was any time, it was now, but it felt weird to blurt it out.

"Long distance would be crazy," Jay agreed. "Especially since you said you don't handle it well."

"My ex and I had to do it for a while because of some training for her job, and it just … Let's just say it made the fine cracks already in our relationship very apparent. Things went south after that pretty fast, and you and I haven't even had any time to be together in person."

"I get it."

"I just … Fuck." Adrian rubbed his forehead. "I know all this shit intellectually but the thought of just walking away from you after this feels wrong."

"I know. It does for me too."

"So, what do we do?"

"I'm willing to give it a shot, if you are." Jay propped his head on one hand. "Besides, there's always texting. And Skype." He shot Adrian a little grin. "When we get lonely."

Adrian chuckled. "There is that." God, was he really considering this?

"I'm actually going to be in Pittsburgh in a few months."

"Really?"

"Yeah, a friend of mine growing up moved there a few years ago. He's getting married." Jay's eyes lit up. "You could be my date. Ever been to a big Indian wedding?"

Adrian shook his head. "I've heard they're pretty amazing."

"This one should be. The groom is planning to ride in on a horse. It's not quite as cool as riding in on an elephant but ..."

"It's still pretty cool," Adrian agreed. "My—I'd like to see that." He'd nearly said, "My daughter would love to see that." She would too. Molly was crazy about horses.

Jay shot him an odd look. Okay, there was no more stalling. If he were going to do this, he needed to tell Jay about his kids now. That could be a huge deal-breaker for him, and if it was, he might as well get it out of the way now. Adrian licked his lips. "I'd like to keep seeing you, but there's—"

The shrill beep of his alarm cut him off. Jay fumbled for the device on the nightstand and handed it to Adrian. He silenced the noise. "Shit. That's me. I've gotta get going. I've got a plane to catch." He still needed to dress, pack, and check out of the hotel.

"We can talk more about logistics later," Jay said. His smile was bright as he looked up at Adrian.

"Yeah, okay."

Adrian had kissed Jay again, deeply, on the sidewalk in front of the hotel an hour later. "Call me when you land?" Jay asked. "Or at least, once you get home?"

"I will," Adrian promised with one final kiss. He turned away, heading toward the train station, but the promise he'd made had begun to feel like a lie as doubts began to crowd in. And by the time he'd reached Pittsburgh, Adrian had already talked himself out of a long-distance relationship.

When Adrian didn't call or text as he'd promised, a few concerned messages and phone calls from Jay had trickled in at first. When the silence stretched on, they grew confused, then increasingly worried. Adrian hadn't responded to any of them. Not even the drunk, angry call where Jay had told him to lose his number.

Eventually the messages went silent, and Adrian didn't hear from him again.

FIVE

Adrian awoke again when the light flicked on in the bathroom. He squinted in the darkness and saw Jay slip into the bathroom, then close the door quietly behind him. Adrian rolled onto his back and stared up at the ceiling. Memories from their weekend in New York bombarded him again.

A wave of sadness swept over Adrian as he thought about the first morning he and Jay had woken up in bed together. That had been the moment he'd fallen for Jay. Not fallen in love, exactly. It had been too soon. Love, real love, took time. But it had been like their souls had connected for a moment. For a brief time, they'd stopped being just Jay and Adrian, two virtual strangers in bed together, and had become something more.

Adrian sat up, his eyes damp, knowing there was no way he'd get back to sleep now. He wiped at his face before he flicked on the light and checked his phone. He had a message from Henry at the bakery. Nothing urgent, just a question about an order, and he fired off a text in response. He was just debating if he should get up and make coffee when Jay opened the bathroom door. He gave Adrian a startled glance.

"Sorry. Didn't mean to wake you."

"It's fine," Adrian said quietly. He glanced at the clock. "Besides, this is sleeping in for me."

Jay cracked a small smile. The first genuine one Adrian had seen from him this weekend. "I'm sure it is."

"When's your interview?"

Jay looked handsome in his slacks and button-down shirt. Professional but approachable. He glanced at the gold watch on his wrist. "Not for a couple of hours but I have to take public transit to get there, and I don't want to be late. I found a coffee shop nearby that I can always kill time in if I get there early."

"I could drive you."

"Nah, that's okay."

"Are you sure? It's the least I can do under the circumstances. Call it a tiny bit of atonement?"

Jay shrugged. "I guess. You can if you really want."

"Yeah, I'm happy to." Adrian scrambled out of bed. "Give me two seconds to get dressed and brush my teeth, and I'll be ready to go."

"If you're driving, you can take at least three." *There.* There was a glimmer of Jay again. Not this cold, shut-down version but the softer, open one Adrian had gotten to know last year.

Adrian laughed as he pulled off his T-shirt.

They both froze, and Jay just blinked at him for a moment. "I'll just ..." Jay cleared his throat. "I'll go make some coffee while you get ready."

Damn it, Adrian had made it awkward again. Still, it was a tiny bit of progress. The smallest amount but he'd take what he could get.

Adrian hurried through his morning routine and met Jay in the kitchen. He'd been quick. The coffee was still brewing, and there were two mugs on the counter.

"Want to send me the address of where we're going while we wait?" Adrian said. "I'll get the GPS all set up on my phone."

Jay nodded, and a moment later, his phone pinged with an address. "It should only take about twenty minutes to get there," Adrian said after he put it into the map.

"Oh, that's not bad," Jay said. The tense set of his shoulders relaxed a little. "Plenty of time to enjoy a cup of coffee before we head out."

"Okay." Adrian's phone blooped at him from the counter, and he picked it up, frowning. A Skype call from his kids. "I've gotta get this real quick."

"Sure," Jay said as Adrian accepted the call.

"Hey there, what are you doing up so early?" Adrian asked as soon as the screen showed his daughter, still dressed in her pajamas with tangled light-brown hair that clearly hadn't been brushed yet.

Molly rubbed her eyes. "Josh wanted breakfast, and Mommy was still sleeping."

"Aww, that was nice of you. What did you make?"

"Microwave oatmeal. It was yummy."

"Nice job, kiddo! That's a solid choice." Adrian smiled at her. "I love that you called me to tell me about your breakfast, but I'm going to have to go in a few minutes. Is there anything you need before I go?"

"No." She yawned. "Just wanted to say hi."

"I'm glad you did. I miss your face."

"I miss you too, Daddy."

"I've gotta go, babycakes. I'm driving a friend to a job interview, okay?"

"K. Say hi to Uncle Seth and Uncle Erik for me."

"I will. Love you. Tell your brother I love him too."

She wrinkled her nose. "Okay."

"I'll call you tonight. I promise. And I'll be home in a few days."

After Adrian finished saying his goodbyes and hung up, he looked over to see Jay staring at him with an inscrutable expression.

"That's, uh, Molly. My eldest. She's eight."

"Cute kid." Apparently, Jay had taken a peek at Adrian's screen. Adrian didn't mind, but he'd wondered why Jay had cared. Maybe he wasn't quite as indifferent as he pretended to be. Or was that just wishful thinking on Adrian's part?

"Uh, yeah, I think so. But I'm a little biased." Plus, everyone always said she looked just like him. Josh took after their mother more.

"Here's your coffee." Jay slid the mug toward him. Adrian lifted it to his lips and took a sip. It already had cream in it. No sugar. Just the way he liked it. Adrian shouldn't be so pleased that Jay had remembered, but he was. He could also see that Jay's cup was already half-gone.

"Thanks." He gulped down a few scalding sips.

After they finished, Adrian rinsed the mugs and spoons before he realized he probably could have just shoved them in the dishwasher. As he dried his hands, he looked back to see Jay scowling at him.

"Shit, sorry, let's get going. I don't want to make you late." Adrian snatched his keys off the counter where he'd left them earlier and shoved his phone in his pocket.

Adrian rushed to lace his sneakers, and they tangled under his clumsy fingers. When he finally stood, he saw Jay had shrugged on a soft-looking leather jacket. Jesus, he was handsome enough as is. In the coat, he was practically lethal. Adrian tried not to stare at Jay's butt as he strode through the parking lot, leading the way.

Adrian failed completely.

They didn't speak much once they were seated in the truck. The restaurant was on the other side of the city, and although traffic had picked up a little since he'd input the location in his phone earlier, a glance at the ETA assured Adrian that Jay should arrive with time to spare. The last thing Adrian wanted to do was screw up this opportunity for Jay.

"Why do they want you there so fucking early?" Adrian said after his third jaw-cracking yawn. The coffee could kick in any minute now as far as he was concerned. "I mean, bakery hours are one thing, but at a fine dining restaurant, it seems weird."

Jay shrugged. "I don't know. The guy said he wanted to get the interview done before everyone started to prep for tonight."

"That makes sense, I guess. You want me to pick you up when you're done?"

"No. I have to hang out for the second one later today, anyway. It's not too far from here. It's right on the bus line, and the bus runs pretty frequently."

"Are you sure? I could run you back there, then," Adrian offered tentatively. "I'm just helping Seth unpack today. Or I could at least pick you up after the second interview."

"It's fine. I've got this." Jay didn't sound hostile, but his tone was firm.

"Okay." Adrian knew not to push anymore. "Good luck!"

Jay nodded once, opened the door, then got out of the truck.

Adrian stared after him a moment, feeling a little deflated. He hadn't expected effusive praise but a thank you would have been nice.

Not that he deserved it.

———

When Adrian returned to the loft, Seth was in the kitchen, wearing pajamas and staring at the coffee maker as if he could will it to brew faster with his mind alone.

"Where've you been?" Seth asked, lifting his head to squint at Adrian. His hair was sticking up in at least eighteen directions, and he sounded a little groggy. Considering the fact that he'd flown in from Barcelona two days ago, Adrian wasn't surprised. Yesterday had been a very long, tiring day, even more so for someone dealing with jet lag.

"Dropping Jay off at his interview." Adrian slipped the spare key Seth had loaned him yesterday into his jean's pocket.

"Oh." Seth looked surprised, and Adrian hardly blamed him. The tension between them had been palpable. "Want some coffee?"

"I've already had one cup, but I wouldn't turn down another."

Once Seth poured the coffee, Adrian carried the mug over to the floor-to-ceiling windows in the living room. The sun was beginning to come up, and the view of the pink-and-orange-washed Philly skyline was amazing. Adrian snapped a few pictures to show Molly and Josh. Which reminded him, he should find a few souvenirs to bring home to them.

"Morning."

Adrian turned to see Erik walk into the kitchen, his red hair darkened from water and his face clean-shaven. Seth sat on one of the stools at the island, and Erik went over to stand between Seth's thighs. Seth reached out and grabbed his hips, pulling him in closer. "You sure you can't play hooky today?" he murmured.

"Unfortunately, no. I have another important meeting. I'm sorry. I wish I could stay home with you."

Seth smiled. "It's okay. You're going to come home to me tonight. And every night after that when I'm not jetting off somewhere."

"I like that thought." Erik leaned in and kissed Seth lightly.

"I like that thought too."

God, Adrian could hear the love for each other in their voices. Damn. He *was* jealous of his brother. Really fucking jealous.

"I made you coffee." Seth pressed a travel mug into Erik's hand with a smile.

"Is it a mocha?"

Seth chuckled. "Maybe. You'll have to find out when you get to work."

"I'm not allowed to drink it until then?"

"Nope."

"You and your rules." Erik's voice was amused. He dipped his head and kissed Seth again. "Guess I better get going, then."

"Guess so." Seth gently pushed him back, then slipped off the stool. "I'll walk you to the door."

There was more murmured conversation between them near the door that Adrian only half-listened to. He heard one part clearly though. "I am crazy in love with you, you know that, right?" Seth said with a little sigh.

"You're not the only one. At all. I love you like crazy too. See you later."

Adrian heard the sound of a kiss, then the door closing.

I could have had that, Adrian thought with a pang. It had certainly felt like the potential for it was there with Jay. They'd just meshed so flawlessly. There had never been a shortage of things to talk about. The chemistry had been scorching, and the intellectual connection just as intense. They'd just ... fit. As if they'd known each other for years. As if they'd been meant to be together.

But it was too late. Adrian couldn't undo the damage he'd already caused. All he could do now was try to apologize and make Jay hate him a little less.

"Hey, you okay?" Seth said as he returned. "You have the saddest look on your face."

"Not really." Adrian stared down into his coffee, his eyes burning a little.

"I'm guessing this has something to do with Jay? You've both been acting weird as fuck since you saw each other. Come on, we're alone now. You can spill."

"Yeah." Adrian sighed and walked over to the couch. "Come on. Sit down for a bit. This is going to take a while."

Seth carried over his mug, then dropped into the chair across from Adrian. "So, what'd you do, sleep together at the expo or something?"

"We didn't do a lot of sleeping," Adrian muttered. "But, yes."

"Oh." Seth's eyes got big. "I was sorta joking."

"Yeah, I wasn't." Adrian let out an even bigger, heavier sigh. "I really fucked up."

"How so?"

"Uhh, well, we had a hell of a weekend together, and then I ghosted him."

Seth grimaced at him. "Well, that was shitty."

"Yeah. Tell me about it." Adrian tilted his head back and stared at the exposed ductwork on the ceiling. "I didn't mean to."

"Does anyone mean to?"

He looked at his brother again. "I don't know. You're talking to someone who never dates."

"So, you're ... bad at it. You can get better."

"Yeah, well, it's too late now."

"With Jay?"

Adrian sighed heavily. "Yeah, he's pissed. And he has every right to be. I was *such* an asshole to him."

"Given how angry Jay still is a year later, there's a chance it might not be too late."

"How do you figure?"

"If he'd stopped caring for you, he'd just ignore you or blow you off. The opposite of love isn't hate, Adrian. It's indifference."

"So how do I fix things with Jay, then?"

"I think you should start by coming up with a way to apologize to him. Big time."

The thought lingered as they finished their coffee, then tackled the huge stack of boxes in the den.

A big apology. Adrian mulled over the idea as he helped Seth unpack and settle his belongings around the loft.

How in the hell do I go about that?

"So why did you ghost Jay in the first place?" Seth asked over lunch. He'd taken Adrian out for what he'd deemed "The Best Philly Cheesesteaks on the planet". After a few bites of the thinly sliced rib-eye beef, melted Provolone, and hoagie roll, Adrian was inclined to agree. "I'm trying to understand this."

"Because I'm an idiot," he said gloomily.

"Yeah, but we know that."

Adrian kicked him under the small table. "You're not helping, asshole."

"Give me something to work with and I will."

Adrian sighed as he set down his sandwich. "I got spooked, I guess."

"Are you sure you just weren't afraid of getting hurt again?"

"I know I am," he admitted. "After the way stuff went down with Michelle, I was pretty gun-shy about relationships."

"You guys are doing better now though, right?"

"We are." The divorce had been rough. They'd tried their best to keep the fighting from spilling out in front of the kids, but he knew they hadn't been able to hide it entirely. "We're cordial now, at least," he admitted. "We talk about the weather and the kids' school stuff when we do drop-offs and all that. The kids come first for both of us."

"Didn't Michelle say she was seeing someone?"

"Yeah. She's got a new boyfriend. He seems decent, and the kids get along with him fine."

"Well, that's encouraging."

"I guess maybe I'm afraid shit will hit the fan if she finds out I'm dating men."

Seth looked surprised. "She never seemed homophobic to me. I mean, I knew her for a lot of years, and she was always really nice to me, and she was friendly to any of the guys I was dating. I never got a whiff of disapproval."

"Yeah, I know. I don't think she's homophobic, per se. Just ... not okay with her ex-husband being bi. She wasn't really okay with her husband being bi either, but that's a whole separate issue."

Seth winced. "Yeah, okay, I can see that. I mean, I don't understand it, but I know some people are like that."

"I'm sure she'll get over it eventually but ..." He sighed.

"But maybe that was another reason you gave up on the idea of something with Jay?"

"Yeah. Maybe." Adrian contemplated the idea. "I hadn't really considered that, but you have a good point. The divorce wasn't even final when I met Jay, so maybe that was somewhere in the back of my head. Wondering if it would impact the custody agreement. Not that it should but ..."

"So maybe you were just kinda rushing things with Jay then," Seth offered.

"Probably. I just ..." Adrian had to swallow past the lump in his throat. "I really liked him. When we were together, it seemed like such a stupid idea to miss out on something great just because of the way we'd met and the distance but ..."

"But maybe your timing was just really off," Seth offered.

"No doubt. But that still doesn't give me a clue how to fix it," Adrian said. "Other than a big apology."

"At the very least, he deserves that," Seth said. "I mean, I love you, Adrian, and you're my brother, but I'm not going to pull any punches. You *were* a dick to him, and I'm not going to cut you slack on that."

"No, I get that. He's your friend. And friend or not, I don't deserve you to go easy on me, anyway. I fucked up. I'll own that."

"So at the bare minimum, tell him how sorry you are. Explain why you fucked up. You can't go anywhere with it until you get that out of the way, at least."

"You're right, you're right."

"I'm always right." Seth shot him a smug smile. "Now, finish your lunch. Your fries are getting cold, and that is way too good a sandwich to let go to waste."

"Yeah, okay." Adrian grabbed a fry. They weren't cold yet, thankfully.

"Besides, you'll need your strength. We still have a shitload more boxes to go through."

Adrian groaned and threw the fry at his brother. "You need to own less crap, dude."

They chatted about less weighty subjects as they finished lunch, but on the walk back to Seth and Erik's place, they fell silent. Seth seemed content just to enjoy the sights, and Adrian was lost in thought.

Seth had given him a lot to think about. For all the shit he'd given Seth over the years about being immature and never really growing up, in this regard, he had Adrian beat. He was clearly doing a hell of a lot better job with relationships than Adrian was. His brother had a fiancé who adored him, and all Adrian had was a failed marriage and a guy he'd had a fling with who was so pissed he'd hardly look at him. Adrian had no room to talk at all.

———

Jay seemed far less tense when he returned from the interviews, windblown and smiling.

"Dude, how'd it go?" Seth clapped him on the arm as soon as he'd opened the door to let him in.

"I'm afraid to get my hopes up, but I feel like it went pretty well at both places," Jay said as he shrugged off his leather jacket. Adrian tried not to stare. Jay's thick black hair had flopped over his forehead, and Adrian quelled the urge to smooth it back. Jay's gaze flicked over to him as if he'd heard Adrian's thoughts. "How'd you guys do?"

"Pretty well." Seth gestured around. "There's art in all sorts of places now, and most of my clothes are hung up. Adrian's been dealing with the kitchen stuff. Of course, Erik might not be crazy about where some of it ended up, but we can move it around if he doesn't like it. At least, it's out of the boxes."

Even Adrian had to admit that Seth's rug from Marrakesh and his art from well, *everywhere*, had made a big improvement in the place. Adrian had done little more in the kitchen than hand wash and dry Seth's handmade pottery bowls and blown glass tumblers and set them all out on the open shelves that lined the kitchen walls, but even that small addition had added some color and life to the stark space.

"This does look nice," Jay said as he walked around the living room, checking out Seth's belongings. "Seriously. This is a great place, and your stuff looks amazing in it."

Seth beamed at him. "It feels weird having my first really grown-up home."

Adrian snorted. "You're thirty-four years old. Isn't it about time?"

"Is it weird being at a different stage of life than your boyfriend? Sorry, fiancé," Jay asked.

Seth shrugged as they all congregated in the kitchen around the large island.

"Sometimes. Meeting his daughter Joanna was weird as hell the first time. But she's pretty cool and more than a decade younger than me, so it's not so bad." He nudged Jay with his elbow. "So, tell us about the interviews. You said they went well, but we want details."

"I definitely liked the first place better than the second," Jay said. "The executive chef seemed really cool and totally unphased when I told him about what happened at The Kensington."

"What did happen?" Adrian blurted out. He'd been dying to know, and he could have googled it, but it felt like an invasion of Jay's privacy even if it was public knowledge. Jay's gaze flicked up to meet his. "I mean, if you don't mind sharing," Adrian amended.

"No, it's fine. I might need a beer for this, though."

"Beer coming up." Seth walked over to the refrigerator. "You want one, Adrian?"

"Why not? We've been working all day."

"That's the spirit."

When they were all seated in the living room, Jay took a long drink from his bottle and looked at Adrian. "So, part of my duties as head pastry chef at the hotel was to manage the ordering and inventory for the desserts. It all ultimately went through the executive chef because he had to sign off on everything that came through the kitchen, but we worked together well. I didn't notice a problem at first. Or, at least, I didn't blame him for the problem. I did notice there were little discrepancies on orders. Different products than what I'd ordered. Different quantities. I made some comment to him about it, and he assured me it was an issue with the supplier. But then I started noticing the products were inferior. I wasn't getting the results I was used to, that sort of thing, and I had some real concerns."

Adrian frowned. Of course, Jay would be concerned. As a baker, if you couldn't count on getting consistent results, that was stressful and bad for business.

"So, I brought it to his attention. He blew me off again, said he'd have a talk with the supplier, but it nagged at me. Something didn't feel right. One day, I noticed he'd left some of the order sheets on his desk. I snuck a peek and noticed some inconsistencies between what I'd told him to order and what he'd actually ordered. To make a very long, sordid story short, I found out he was up to some really shady business to line his pocket. Basically, he was skimming from the hotel. I gathered as much evidence as I could and took it to the general manager of the hotel. She believed me, and she was great about it. She fired him, and I thought it was going to be fine, but the new executive chef said he wanted to start with a fresh slate, and I got let go. I got a decent severance but looking for new positions has been a nightmare."

"Because the assumption is that you were let go because of what happened," Adrian said.

"Yes." Jay dragged a hand through his hair. "My name is tied to it now, so even when I explain the situation, they don't want someone tainted by it. It's a nightmare."

"That's terrible. Especially after you did the right thing by turning the executive chef in. I'm so sorry." Adrian laid a hand on Jay's shoulder. He flinched in surprise, and Adrian pulled his hand away. "Sorry," he muttered again but this time for a very different reason.

"Which is why I'm in Philly looking for jobs," Jay said. He took a long pull from his drink. "I'm ready to get the hell out of New York if it means I can start fresh."

"Well, you have three different places you have interviews at," Seth said cheerfully. "We'll find you something."

"I hope so. I don't know what I'll do, otherwise." Jay's mouth turned down at the corners. It broke Adrian's heart to see him looking so gloomy and despondent. In the, admittedly short time Adrian had known him, he'd been such an upbeat, positive guy. But a situation like that could bring anyone down.

"I'm sorry I brought it up," Adrian said.

"It's fine." Jay sighed. "Either something will work out here or I'll keep looking. I'll move to Seattle or L.A. or something, if I need to."

"Okay." Seth stood. "That's enough moping. There are still boxes to unpack."

"Forced manual labor. You really know how to cheer a guy up," Adrian said as he stood. He heard a small snort that he assumed came from his brother, but when he glanced over, he caught a glimpse of a small smile on Jay's face, and that made him feel good. It was another tiny crack in Jay's armor. He smiled to himself as he walked toward the open box on the floor that he'd been dealing with earlier. All Adrian had to do was keep slowly working his way back into Jay's good graces. If he softened Jay up a little, it would hopefully give him an opportunity for them to sit down and have a good conversation.

An opening was all he needed.

Seth appeared a moment later with several boxes. He set them down with a groan. "Hey, why don't you help Adrian take care of this stuff, Jay? It's all for the dining room. You can unpack it and set it all out on the table."

Jay hesitated a second, then nodded. "Sure, whatever you need. Let me go change out of my interview clothes."

Ten minutes later, Jay returned, wearing jeans that cupped his butt nicely and a T-shirt that stretched perfectly across his toned chest. They got to work as Adrian wracked his brain for what to say to break the awkward silence. Surprisingly, Jay was the one who spoke first.

"Wow."

Adrian glanced up to see him examining a wine bottle opener that appeared to have a carved handle. "Wow is right." He stepped a little closer. "Mind if I ...?" He held out a hand, and Jay passed it over. He rubbed his thumb across the wood. "That's incredible."

"It is," Jay agreed. "I wonder where he got this."

"I don't know, but I'm going to have to give my brother shit for not getting me one for Christmas or my birthday. I mean, I don't drink a lot of wine, but that's not the point."

"Your birthday is only a few weeks away, right?" Jay said. "There's still time."

Adrian looked at him in surprise. He'd remembered Adrian's birthday. That was interesting. "Yeah, on the 28th of February."

Jay's was August 3rd, if Adrian remembered right.

"Yeah, I remembered because it was almost leap year, right?"

"Yes. Exactly."

"Anyway, maybe your brother will still get you a fancy wooden wine bottle opener."

Adrian chuckled. "Maybe. He got me Penn State season tickets for Christmas, so I shouldn't complain."

"You definitely shouldn't!" Seth said. Adrian looked up to see him deposit another box on the floor nearby. "I am an *awesome* brother."

"Minus the forced labor, yes, you are."

SIX

Pleased with how much they'd gotten done today and the slight softening in Jay, Adrian whistled a little under his breath as he walked from the bathroom into the bedroom later that evening and came face to face with the man he'd just been thinking about.

"Oh." They both stopped in their tracks. Jay's gaze stayed fixed on Adrian's bare chest for a moment before he looked up. "Sorry. I thought you were still helping Seth in the den. I came in to change for dinner."

"No, uh, I was showering. I wanted to clean up before we all headed out. I was just about to get dressed." Jay's gaze was so intent. It flustered him but, God, he *liked* having Jay look at him that way again.

"Right. Yeah, of course." Jay cleared his throat. "I should leave you to that."

"You don't ... have to." Adrian rested a hand on the edge of his towel, right near the knot. "You've seen it all before, right?"

"I … yeah. I have." Jay seemed to shake himself, and his expression turned stern. He stepped forward into Adrian's space. "What are you trying to do? Seduce me into forgiving you?"

"Well, I was originally planning on a big apology. Starting to think this might be more effective, though." The way Jay looked at him gave him the courage to be bold. Either that or make the second biggest mistake of his life. He wasn't quite sure.

"You might be right." Jay wet his lips.

Adrian cocked an eyebrow at him. "Why do I feel like we're playing a game of chicken here?"

"Who said anything about playing chicken?" Jay mirrored his expression as he crossed his arms. "I'm not stopping you."

Adrian swallowed nervously as he checked to be sure the bedroom door was shut. Okay, so he was the only one considering chickening out. This felt … weird. And like it was probably the absolute riskiest way to go about getting Jay to forgive him. But Jay was definitely looking at him with heat in his eyes, and well, Adrian had missed the hell out of that. Besides, at this point, what did he have to lose?

With his gaze locked on Jay's, Adrian worked the knot loose and let the towel drop to the floor. For a moment, Jay just stared at Adrian's face. He didn't follow the path of the towel or do anything but look into Adrian's eyes, and that was almost worse. More intimate. It rattled Adrian.

But then Jay's gaze moved down. Slowly—so slowly—across his chest, his abs, and finally to his groin where it lingered.

"You've been working out."

"Yeah," Adrian said hoarsely. "Gotta counteract all the baked goods somehow."

"Stroke it for me."

"What?"

"Stroke yourself for me. I want to watch."

"Um." Adrian blinked. "Okay?" That was the last thing he'd expected. Jay ordering him to give him a blowjob? Sure. Or maybe bending him over the bed and fucking him hard in punishment. But not this. Definitely not this.

Adrian's awkwardness must have shown as he wrapped a hand around his cock and slowly stroked. He half-expected Jay to tell him to stop but he didn't. Just nodded at him. "Nice. Keep going."

So Adrian did. The nerves and awkwardness faded as his arousal grew, and it wasn't long before he was hard and leaking at the tip. He spat in his hand, then smoothed it down the shaft to slick his way. Jay's eyes were dark and intense as he stared at Adrian's hand as it flew over his cock, moving faster and faster. Desire built in Adrian quickly, leaving him breathless.

"I'm getting close," Adrian said, his voice tight and thin as he fought to hold his release back.

"So come." It wasn't really an order, more of a dare, but the words and the intent way Jay watched were more than enough to send Adrian tumbling over the edge a few strokes later.

With a groan, Adrian came into his hand, barely managing to catch it, but a few drops leaked from his fist and fell to the floor. He panted for a moment as his head swam from the orgasm. After he steadied himself, he swiped the towel from the floor to scrub his hand and the hardwood clean. Thank God, it wouldn't leave a stain on the floor. He *really* didn't want to explain that to his brother.

He stood to see Jay still watching Adrian's every move. Jay's eyes glittered darkly, and there was no mistaking the rapid rise and fall of his chest. Jay had been turned on by Adrian's display.

"Should I?" Adrian gestured to the clear arousal in Jay's trousers.

"No. I'm good." Jay's lips curved up in a little smile. "That's exactly what I wanted."

He disappeared into the bathroom a moment later, and Adrian sat down hard on the edge of the bed, his head spinning with a mix of pleasure and confusion. *What the hell just happened?*

Someone banging on the bedroom door made Adrian's heart leap in this throat, and he turned to stare at it, wide-eyed.

"Hey, you just about ready?" his brother called.

"Yeah," Adrian hollered back hoarsely. "Just give me a few."

Adrian finished cleaning up, then dug through his bag for something to wear. He hadn't brought any dress clothes, but he picked out a pair of nicer jeans and a burgundy zip-up sweater that he thought looked pretty decent. By the time Jay came out of the bathroom, Adrian was fixing his hair in front of the full-length mirror. From the way his gaze flickered over Adrian's body, he approved. It sent a surge of pleasure through Adrian. This wasn't how he'd anticipated things going with Jay, but he'd work with whatever he got.

Hopefully, jerking off in front of Jay had broken the ice, and they could talk later. All Adrian could do was hope.

———

They walked to a Brazilian steakhouse that Seth and Erik had been raving about for a while. It had begun to snow, so Adrian was grateful the restaurant was only a few blocks away.

February weather in Pennsylvania, Adrian thought. *So fickle.*

The restaurant was warm, though, and after they shed their coats and ordered drinks, Adrian snuck several glances at Jay, who sat across from him, handsome in a black button-down shirt. God, he looked incredible. All Adrian wanted to do was lean over, grab Jay by the back of the neck, and kiss the hell out of him.

"So, how does the churrasco sound?" Seth asked. "I was thinking we could all get that. You'll have a chance to try everything that way."

They all agreed to follow his suggestion. Adrian was looking forward to indulging in the unlimited tableside service of fire-roasted meat and as many trips as they wanted to the market bar where they could fill their plates with a variety of Brazilian side dishes.

Although every bite Adrian put in his mouth was delicious, he spent at least half of dinner thinking about jerking off in front of Jay earlier. Why had he wanted to see that? To somehow humiliate Adrian? It hadn't been humiliating, though. It had been hot. Really hot. He'd enjoyed it. And clearly Jay had too. So what angle was he working?

It made him sad to even consider the idea that Jay might be working an angle at all. He had never struck Adrian as that type before. He hadn't seemed like the kind of guy who would try to manipulate things to go to his advantage. But the truth was, they'd only known each other for a few days, and there was probably a lot Adrian didn't know about him.

And, well, Adrian had hurt him. He deserved whatever Jay wanted to dish out at him.

He glanced over at Jay, who was laughing at something Erik had just said. It was nice to see him looking more relaxed and happy, but his good mood made Adrian even more baffled. Adrian had been the one to orgasm, not Jay. If anyone should be feeling good right now, it was him. But he was strung tighter than ever. God, this was all so damn confusing. He just hoped at some point it would begin to make sense again.

"Shit, I'm such a bad Hindu," Jay said a bit later, slicing into his steak as he nodded toward his cocktail.

Seth chuckled. "Your mother would be appalled. Beef and liquor." He made a tsking sound.

"She really would." Jay took a bite and chewed. "And she doesn't know half of what I do."

Adrian remembered their previous conversations about the line Jay skirted between being the good Indian son his parents expected and the man he wanted to be. It must be tough.

Erik glanced at him. "We could have gone somewhere else if you wanted," he said with a concerned frown.

Jay waved it off. "No, I was the one who told Seth I wanted to come here. He's been raving about it since you guys tried it out for the first time. I'm thoroughly enjoying myself so don't feel bad on my account."

"The food is incredible, and I figured you and Adrian would appreciate it," Seth said. "I promise I won't tell your mother you indulged in an orgy of meat."

Adrian nearly choked on his own bite of steak.

Erik looked pained. "I don't think that quite came out the way you meant it, Seth."

"Didn't it?" Seth gave his fiancé a cheeky wink before turning back to Jay. "No, seriously, though. I understand your parents have their values and expectations, but it's your life, Jay."

"It is." He set down his fork and knife with a little sigh. "It's hard, though. I think that's part of why I like the idea of getting out of New York."

"Because of your parents?" Seth asked.

"I love them, but ... they want me to be someone I'm not. They've accepted a lot of the decisions I've made, but that doesn't mean they aren't disappointed. And that's pretty heavy to carry around."

Adrian quelled the urge to reach across the table and touch Jay's arm, reassure him. Seth's gaze flickered over to Adrian as if he'd somehow heard Adrian's thoughts, then rested his hand on Jay's back in silent support. "I'm sure it is."

"I've experienced that," Erik said. Adrian glanced over at him. "My father was a very rigid man. I don't think he even *tried* to understand that I wanted different things than he did."

"At least, then you can be pissed and call him an asshole," Jay pointed out.

Erik chuckled. "True."

"I can't even be mad at my parents. I get it. They feel like my choices are a repudiation of their culture, and that *has* to hurt." Jay sighed. "I don't mean to hurt them. Ever. But the things I choose to do to make myself happy are hurtful to them. I think we've reached the 'don't ask, don't tell' stage of our relationship, but I never stop feeling like I have to watch everything I say."

"How so?"

Jay glanced up at Adrian as if surprised he'd spoken. He'd been pretty quiet since they sat down. "Well, I don't talk a whole lot about my dating life with my dad. I don't talk about work with my mom. And I certainly don't talk about the fact that I eat beef or drink liquor with either of them. If I don't talk about it, they don't ask, and we're all happier because they can pretend I'm not doing any of these horrible things that take me away from being a good Hindu. But the closer I live to them and the more often I see them, the harder that illusion is to maintain. I'm hoping if I move a little farther away, there will be less friction."

"So, what do you think will happen when you meet a man you fall in love with?" Erik asked, taking a sip of his drink.

"I don't know," Jay said. "I do know if I have to be gay, my mom would prefer I'm in a settled relationship. She's been cordial to a couple of men I've introduced to the family. I'm not sure how they really feel about it, but I know she'd feel better about telling her friends that her son has a husband rather than a string of casual men."

"Do you think she actually says that?" Seth sounds surprised.

Jay snorted. "No, I think she tells them I'm busy with my work and don't have time to find a husband. But people probably assume the worst. Getting me married off would save face."

"That's a big burden on you," Erik said thoughtfully.

"It can be."

A waiter appeared with a skewer of meats, and the relieved look on Jay's face made Adrian realize how heavily this conversation was weighing on Jay.

"Hey, before I forget, do you think you could get that lentil curry recipe from your mom for me?" Seth asked when the waiter was gone. Adrian wanted to kick his brother for bringing the conversation back to Jay's family.

"The *bisi bele bhath* we had the last time you were over? Sure." Jay took a sip of his drink. "But she'll probably be mad you didn't come get it from her yourself before you left."

Seth winced. "I know. Tell her I'm sorry. Things just got crazy with the trip to Spain and the move."

"You know Jay's family?" Adrian asked, surprised.

"Yeah, Jay's parents stopped by the apartment one time, and we started talking about my travel. His mom was adamant I needed to go to India as soon as possible. Don't get me wrong, I'd love to, but I just don't always have a lot of say in where work sends me. Anyway, she made me promise I'd talk to her before I take any trip there so she can give me suggestions of where to visit. And to get in contact with her relatives when I'm there."

"My mom absolutely loves Seth," Jay said. "She was so surprised when she found out he was gay. She kept saying, 'But he's so handsome, he could date any girl he liked,' and I kept having to remind her that he didn't want any girls. After that finally sunk in, she kept asking me if I was dating him. And when I told her I wasn't, she kept asking why not and inviting Seth to dinner. And when he came to dinner, she kept trying to set us up."

"So, I brought Erik with me," Seth said with a laugh.

"It was good, though," Jay said. "The more gay couples my parents meet, the easier time they have with it. Seeing you two together helped, I think."

"Well, I'm glad we could help," Erik said. "I'm going to miss visiting your family. Your mom's cooking is incredible. I'm actually the one who's been bugging Seth to get that recipe from her."

They all laughed.

"Your mom doesn't mind the idea of you dating a white guy?" Adrian asked, surprised.

Jay shrugged. "Lesser of two evils, maybe? Marriage potential is the biggest factor. I know she'd prefer an Indian guy, but she'll take what she can get. There was one white guy I dated who she really liked, especially after he asked her for her recipe for *adrak ki chai*. It's a fairly simple ginger tea but it's my absolute favorite, and it was a really sweet gesture on his part. And it won him major points with my mom."

Jesus, Adrian hoped that Jay had never mentioned Adrian's bad behavior to his mother. Not that he was overly optimistic about repairing things with Jay enough to get involved again—that ship had probably sailed—but he hated the thought of Jay's family thinking badly of him. He didn't like thinking badly of himself. He'd always considered himself a standup guy. He'd never cheated on his taxes—much less, his spouse or someone he was dating. He tried to be kind to everyone he encountered and to teach his kids to do the same. He thought of himself as a good guy, and it didn't sit well with him that he clearly hadn't been when it came to the situation with Jay.

He had some serious atoning to do, and he wondered if he'd made another massive error earlier with Jay when he jerked off in front of him. What had seemed like a promising step forward was now beginning to feel like a mistake.

Fuck.

———

After they finished the meal, Adrian was stuffed. "You're going to have to roll me back to your place," he groaned as he pushed back from the table and stood.

"Same." Jay adjusted his waistband. "I may or may not have had to loosen my belt when I was in the bathroom earlier."

Erik chuckled. "Shall we take the long way home then?"

"Probably a good idea," Seth said. "Unless the temperature has dropped further."

To Adrian's surprise, it was warmer outside than when they'd come in. The snow was still coming down, but they were fat, fluffy flakes that seemed to blanket the world and make it cozy. Some shops were still open, and the streetlights glowed warmly.

"This must be pretty around Christmas," Adrian said to Jay. Seth and Erik walked side by side, and he and Jay had fallen into step behind them.

Jay looked around. "Yeah, I'd imagine so."

"Will you miss New York if you move here?"

"I don't know. I've never lived anywhere but New York. I lived in a Desi neighborhood in Queens growing up, then I moved around Queens and Brooklyn most of my adult life. I'm sure there will be an adjustment period."

"I've always lived in Pittsburgh."

"Would you consider moving?"

"It would be hard. The bakery and the kids have me tied there pretty solidly."

"Yeah." Jay stuffed his hands in his pockets. "I get that."

"I'm sorry, you know?"

"About?"

"A lot of things. Everything I did wrong after we met."

"I don't want to go there, Adrian." Jay sounded tired. "Honestly, the past year has been shit for me. It was like once you ghosted me, everything else in my life blew up in my face. My career went to hell, I've had no luck finding anything new, and my parents are on my case about changing my career now. I'm just fucking tired, and I don't have the energy to hash this out with you right now."

"I'm sorry."

He sighed. "I appreciate you taking responsibility for what you did, but I'm not blaming you for everything else that has gone wrong in my life."

"I can still be sorry you're having to deal with it all at once." They walked in silence a moment. "I have a question though. I thought you said your dad was proud of your career."

"He used to be." There was a sad, wry twist to Jay's mouth when Adrian glanced over at him. "But once I lost my job and got tainted by the scandal ..." He shrugged. "It's hard for my parents to hold up their heads in their community and with the rest of the family when their son is failing at every aspect of his life."

Adrian's heart ached. "I felt like a huge failure when I got divorced. My parents have been married forever. I couldn't even make it ten years." He and Michelle had only managed eight and only the first two had been really good.

"But you're happier now, right?"

"Much." Adrian said firmly. "But that's my point. Yeah, this is a low point for you, but maybe things will turn around and start to look up. They certainly have for me." Well, except for relationships. He was still failing there. But one step at a time, right?

"I guess all I can do is hope my luck turns around, then."

"No, it's not just waiting for your luck to turn around," Adrian argued. "You're here, looking for new opportunities. You're trying to make your own luck. That has to count for something."

"Thanks, Adrian." Jay sounded genuinely grateful. "I think I needed to hear that."

———

"That was a nice walk," Adrian said as they shook the snow off their coats in Erik and Seth's entryway.

"Feeling a little less stuffed?" Seth teased.

"Yes."

"Good because we have dessert."

Jay let out a pained little groan. "What is this? Are you planning to stuff us like geese and make pate of our livers?"

"I can honestly say the thought has never crossed my mind," Seth said, wide-eyed. "I do like pate, but I'm really fucking concerned that you leaped to that conclusion."

Adrian chuckled. "Can the dessert wait until tomorrow?"

"I suppose." Seth looked disappointed. "I was excited about it, though."

"Why? You don't bake."

"I didn't make it." Seth's disappointment turned to exasperation. "That *would* be a disaster."

"Yeah, I remember the last time you tried baking. How did you make a cake that was simultaneously burned on the outside, yet raw in the middle? It should be scientifically impossible."

"If you two could stop squabbling a minute." Erik settled one hand on Adrian's shoulder and another on Seth's. "What Seth is trying to say is that on my way home tonight, I picked up cakes to do a cake tasting. We'd like you and Jay to help us choose our wedding cake flavors."

"Damn it, I can't fight that," Jay said with a resigned sounding sigh.

"No, me either," Adrian agreed. "Bring on the cake!"

"So this one we definitely want unless it somehow tastes bad," Erik said a few minutes later as they sat at the big marble island. He pointed at a slice in the cardboard box. "Chocolate torte with coffee-meringue buttercream, Kalua ganache, and hazelnut mousse."

"Why?" Jay asked.

Adrian groaned. "You haven't heard their adorable little meet-cute story where they fell in love over Seth's special mochas?"

"No." Jay looked between Adrian and Seth. "I heard Erik was an asshole to Seth at first, but Seth somehow won him over. I assumed it involved sex, so I didn't ask to hear any more about it."

"Oh, there was *definitely* sex involved," Seth said with a coy little grin.

Adrian mimed plugging his ears. Seth swatted his hand away. "Oh, I'm not going into detail about the sex. I was just going to tell you about the mochas."

Jay gave him a skeptical look. "They aren't kinky mochas, are they?"

"Jesus. No!" Erik, who had been oddly silent during this whole exchange, protested. "I've told this story to my daughter. When we were staying at the Williamsville Inn, Seth knew I was in a bad mood, so he took shitty hotel coffee, mixed in hot cocoa, and added a splash of bourbon. It was so delicious it warmed even this Grinch's heart." He pointed to himself.

"You've never seemed like a Grinch to me," Jay protested.

"That's because you didn't know me pre-Seth." Erik grinned.

"So this cake is an homage to that?" Adrian waved his fork at the slice of cake they'd been discussing.

"It is!" Seth beamed. "It was Erik's idea too. Turns out the Grinch is a total romantic. Whod've thought?"

Erik ducked his head. "Can we just shut up and eat some cake?"

"Yes." Seth moaned around his first forkful. "Oh-em-gee. This is so good."

"I know." Erik looked equally orgasmic as he savored his bite of cake, and Adrian had to look anywhere but at his face. He did *not* want to think about his brother's fiancé that way.

"What do you think?" Seth looked between Adrian and Jay. "You're the professionals."

"It's good," Jay said carefully as he set his fork down.

"It is. It could be better though, right?" Adrian looked at Jay.

"You think so?" Seth looked surprised.

"Yeah." Jay gave the cake a contemplative look. "I think, personally, I'd go for a slightly more bitter cocoa in the cake to offset the sweetness of the ganache and the mousse."

"I like that." Adrian pointed a fork at him before he turned it on his brother. "And why doesn't this cake have bourbon in it, if you're trying to recreate your meet-cute drink?"

Seth shrugged. "The bakery said they couldn't do it."

In unison, Jay and Adrian shook their heads.

"That's bullshit," Jay said. "They can. They just don't feel like doing it."

Adrian agreed. "A bourbon mousse is totally doable."

"You don't think they should just swap the Kahlua in the ganache for bourbon?" Jay looked surprised.

"Why keep the Nutella mousse?" Adrian countered. "It has no part in their story and it doesn't add anything to this cake."

"Hmm." Jay took another forkful. "I'm not sure I agree. I like the nuttiness."

"What about another nut, like pecan?"

"So a dark chocolate torte with coffee-meringue buttercream, Kalua ganache, and bourbon-pecan mousse?" Jay asked.

"Too much?"

Jay hummed thoughtfully. "Not necessarily. I'd certainly try it both ways and see which I liked better."

"Yeah, I don't think this bakery is going to be up for that," Seth said drily.

"That begs the question, why are we tasting cakes from a bakery in Philly when you're getting married near Buffalo, New York?"

"Well, they have locations in both places. It seemed easiest when I didn't have a lot of time to go to Buffalo to plan things."

"It's a chain?" The disdain dripped from Adrian's lips before he could stop it.

"You make fun of me for being pretentious but you're such a snob," Seth hooted. "Dude, seriously. You just *sneered*."

"I probably am a snob, but if you're looking for something more customized, you won't get that from a chain," Adrian argued.

"He's not wrong."

Adrian smiled at Jay for backing him up.

"They have like, four locations, so that's not much of a chain. But okay, cake snobs. Do *you two* want the job?" Seth said, sounding exasperated. "You're more than welcome to collaborate and make our wedding cake instead if you're going to bitch about our choice of bakers."

Adrian exchanged glances with Jay. He'd almost think his brother had arranged this as a way to nudge them together, but Seth hadn't known that he and Jay knew each other—much less about the rift between them—until yesterday. Seth was crafty but he wasn't that good.

"I ... I mean, I could," Adrian offered. "If you're on board, Jay. And if you both want it." He waved at Seth and Erik.

"Why wouldn't I want my brother to make my wedding cake?" Seth asked. "You're an amazing baker, Adrian. Of course, I'd want you to do it. I didn't ask because, A: I didn't want you to feel obligated, and B: I didn't know how that would work with the distance."

"Well, I'd want to see what kind of kitchen facilities the hotel has before I decide for sure. I could do it at my bakery if I have to but I'd prefer not to drive a cake from Pittsburgh to Buffalo. I'd rather get there a little early and make it on site, if that's possible."

"Well, the kitchens at the hotel were just updated top to bottom," Erik said. "The facilities were totally unusable before, so the hotel didn't even have any dining option. We just finished a total gut job on them, and the restaurant will open soon."

"I think the whole reason he did the renovation was because he was feeling salty about having to walk to nearby restaurants during the snowstorm we were stuck in. All that snow and salt ruined his fancy Italian leather shoes," Seth teased. "But the new kitchen *does* look amazing. I think it'll wow even you two." He waved in Adrian and Jay's general direction.

"Well, as long as I have access to this new and amazing kitchen ..." Adrian said.

Erik chuckled. "I think, as the owner, I should be able to swing that."

"So that just leaves you, Jay," Adrian said. He turned to look at Jay, knowing this might very well blow up in his face. "I can do the cakes by myself, if you'd like, but I'd love your help, if you're interested in collaborating with me."

Jay studied his face for a moment before he nodded. "Sure. Let's make Erik and Seth the best damn wedding cake ever."

SEVEN

Adrian awoke early the next morning. The room was dim, but after Adrian slipped on his glasses, he could see Jay was sprawled on his stomach on the air mattress across the room, sleeping deeply. He was shirtless and his pajama pants rested low on his hips. Adrian remembered kissing his way down Jay's spine, lingering in the small of his back until Jay begged him to continue.

But that had been a year ago, and while Jay seemed to have softened a little, he had made no move toward Adrian after the cake tasting last night. If not for the weird moment before dinner where he challenged Adrian to masturbate in front of him, Adrian might have thought Jay wasn't attracted to him at all anymore.

But one weird voyeuristic moment didn't mean anything else would happen in the future, so Adrian had no idea where they stood. And with thoughts like that whirling around in his head, there was no way he was going to fall asleep again. He got out of bed as quietly as possible, then rummaged through his bag for clothes. He changed in the bathroom and did a cursory job of splashing his face with water and brushing his teeth.

Adrian frowned at his beard in the mirror—it was looking a bit overgrown and scraggly, which wasn't his best look—but he'd left his clippers at home, and he would only be here a few more days. Not worth asking Seth to borrow some. Besides, there was a chance his brother might have used them on other body parts. Adrian shuddered at the thought.

Jay stirred when he left the bathroom, flipping onto his back and squinting up at Adrian. "... time is it?" His voice was thick and a little slurred.

"Early still," Adrian whispered. "Go back to sleep."

"K." Jay turned onto his side, pulling the covers up farther as he buried his face against the pillow.

Adrian stood there looking down at him with a small smile on his face for a moment before he turned and left the room as quietly as possible. Seeing Jay sleep like that, relaxed and vulnerable, brought up so many weird feelings for him. Namely, nostalgia and regret. He missed the man he'd spent that incredible weekend with and cursed himself for wrecking the opportunity they'd had. Even if it had all gone disastrously wrong as they tried to navigate a long-distance relationship, Adrian should have *tried*. He shouldn't have given up without even giving it a chance.

And, more than ever, he regretted that he'd played a major part in what sounded like a horrible year for Jay. He could have been there for Jay, supporting him through a very tough time instead of being a bitter memory that only made Jay feel worse about his life.

What an asshole he'd been.

"What has you looking so melancholy?"

Erik sat at the counter with papers spread out in front of him and a mug of coffee in his hand. Adrian blinked at him, realizing that he'd walked into the kitchen without paying any attention to his surroundings.

Coffee, that's a good idea. Adrian walked to the counter and reached for a pottery mug from one of the open shelves. "Did my brother tell you what happened between Jay and me?"

"Only that you were involved previously, and it hadn't ended well."

"That's the gist of it," Adrian said as he poured himself coffee from the half-full pot. "But I appreciate my brother trying to make me sound like less of a jerk than I was."

Erik chuckled. "We all make mistakes."

"What if your mistakes cost you someone you could see a future with?"

"It almost did." Erik took a sip of his coffee. "I almost let Seth slip away. We'd spent several incredible days together, but when he asked me to come celebrate Christmas with your family, I turned him down. After we walked away from each other at the airport, I had no way to get ahold of him. I came this close to never seeing him again." Erik held his fingers millimeters apart.

"But you didn't break Seth's heart in the process."

"No, I didn't," Erik acknowledged. "Obviously, the situations aren't exactly the same, but I think if something is meant to be, there will be an opportunity to repair it, even if it doesn't seem obvious at first. I certainly don't think you should give up."

"Give up on what?"

Adrian turned to see his brother standing in the entrance to the kitchen, sporting pajamas, some major bedhead, and a wide yawn.

"Things with Jay," Adrian said softly.

"Oh." Seth shuffled sleepily over to Erik, who put an arm around him and drew him down onto his lap.

The ease and casual affection made Adrian's heart ache. He wanted that. With Jay.

"You think it's hopeless," Adrian said.

"No." Seth ran a hand through his wild hair. "I don't think it's hopeless. I *do* think it's going to be tough. There's a difference."

But before they could discuss it any further, Adrian's phone buzzed with a semi-urgent question from Henry at the bakery, and while Adrian responded, Seth went off to pull himself together. By the time Adrian hung up his call, Seth had re-appeared, fully dressed and with neatly-styled hair rather than a mop on his head. Jay was just a few steps behind him.

"Would you like me to make breakfast before we start unpacking more boxes?" Adrian asked.

"That would be great." Erik frowned down at the stacks of papers on the island. "Do you need me to clean this up first?"

Adrian looked across the massive expanse of marble and snorted. "No, I think I have plenty of room to work around it." There were still acres of countertop free.

Jay let out a little snort too. "Yeah, I think you could fit the entire kitchen Seth and I had in the space this island takes up."

"Isn't it glorious?" Seth grinned. "Although, I don't actually have a clue what you're doing, Erik. What is all this paperwork anyway?"

Erik frowned. "It's a bunch of old stuff that belonged to my father. I inherited it all after he died and meant to go through it at the time, but that's about when things went to hell in my marriage, and I just shoved it all in a box. I'm sorry. I'd planned to have it all done before you moved in, Seth, but work has been crazy."

"It's fine." Seth kissed him briefly. "You can go through it today while Jay and Adrian help me unpack. Now, what's for breakfast?"

Adrian, who had been examining the contents of the refrigerator, pulled out a carton of eggs and a slab of bacon. "Assuming you don't mind me helping myself, I was thinking of scrambled eggs, bacon, and toast."

"You bought me that bacon I love?" Seth's eyes went wide, and he kissed Erik soundly on the cheek. "Oh, you do love me!"

"Of course, I do."

Adrian rolled his eyes and glanced at Jay, expecting to see him looking equally disgusted by their sappy behavior, but he was staring at them with an expression that could only be described as wistful.

———

"You're not going to believe what I found, Seth!" Erik called out later that day.

"What?"

"Come in here," Erik replied. "You too, Adrian and Jay."

Adrian stood, stretching his shoulders before they all trooped back into the kitchen, then congregated around the island where Erik stood clutching a handful of papers.

"What did you find?" Seth slid underneath Erik's arm and stared down at what Erik held.

"Here. Look." Erik handed them to Seth, who looked them over, a frown marring his forehead as he scrutinized them intently.

Adrian looked over at Erik. "When you said you owned the hotel near Buffalo, I guess I didn't realize you had inherited it. And what is this mystery you're talking about?"

Erik sighed. "So, the short version of it all is that my father was one of the owners and founders of the property management company I run. He was a bastard. Blatantly cheated on my mom, tried to screw her out of alimony once she finally had enough of his shit ... Just generally, the last person I wanted to emulate. Well, Bertram, my *business partner*"—he looked pointedly at Seth—"discovered last year that my father had purchased The Williamsville Inn decades ago. It was all done very oddly. Through several shell corporations and clearly meant to be kept hidden. I could never figure out *why*. I always assumed it was something he'd bought for a mistress or to hide assets from my mother, but what I just found puts a very different spin on it."

"Take a look," Seth said. "This is really interesting." Adrian peered over Seth's shoulder at a sun-bleached black and white photo. A small boy stood beside a little girl with blonde curls. They held hands in a courtyard.

"That's my father," Erik explained, pointing to the small boy. "According to the caption on the back, this particular photo was taken in 1953, and that little girl is the daughter of the original owner of the inn. There are several photos that indicate he used to spend time there as a kid. Over a number of summers."

"Hmm. He's more sentimental than I would have expected," Seth said. "I mean, if he held onto these photos all this time ..."

"Yes. Far more sentimental than I realized," Erik admitted. "He certainly never showed that side to my mother or me."

Seth set the photos on the counter, then held up other papers. "Look, there are all these postcards and letters too. Did you read all of them?"

Erik nodded. "Yes. They all seem to be between this girl, Grace Howard, and my father. They wrote to each other for years. It trailed off once they were teenagers and stopped completely when they reached adulthood, but it started up again later in their lives. Apparently, Grace contacted him to let him know her parents had died, and she was selling the inn. She thought he might be interested in owning it."

"Huh," Jay said.

Adrian glanced over, realizing that Jay was next to him, their arms pressed together as they both tried to see the papers Seth was still reading.

"Listen to this," Seth said. "'I'm glad you contacted me, Grace. I have such happy memories of the place. I'd hate to see it sold and torn down. Give me a week or so and I'll make a trip to Buffalo to take a look at the inn. If it seems like a viable financial asset, I'll consider purchasing it.'" Seth shuffled some papers. "And this. 'I've decided to purchase the inn. While it may not be the smartest financial decision I've ever made, walking through the place brought back so many memories. I can't allow it to be sold to a developer. Your asking price is reasonable. I've included the contract. Please review it and get back to me.'"

"The man was cutthroat in business," Erik said. "The fact that he was willing to pay full price was entirely out of character for him. Anyone else he would have bargained into the ground, and if they wouldn't go as low as he wanted, he would have walked away from the deal."

"This is all fascinating," Jay said.

"It is," Seth agreed. "Let me keep reading, though. This is from Grace to Erik's father. 'Dear Karl, I so enjoyed your visit. I was sorry to hear about your marriage. The pictures of your son that you showed me were wonderful. He's grown to be quite a handsome young man. Although, I'm sad to let the place go, I can't tell you how relieved I am to know that the inn will be in your hands. My husband's health doesn't allow us to remain in Buffalo. The weather in Arizona will be far more beneficial to him. He is the most important thing to me, but it puts my mind at ease to know the inn will continue to be run under your watchful eye. I trust you to find a caretaker who can be relied on to look after the place on a daily basis. Thank you again. As soon as we have a permanent address in Arizona, I'll share it with you. I wish you the best and can't thank you enough for what you've done. Fondly, Grace.'"

"But why keep it a secret?" Adrian asked, frowning as he tried to put all the pieces together. "I mean, were the shell corporations really necessary? The purchase seems straightforward enough otherwise."

Erik shrugged. "The man hated the thought of anyone perceiving him as weak. Maybe he didn't like the idea of people knowing he'd acquired it for sentimental reasons?"

"I suppose that's possible," Seth said, sounding skeptical. Privately, Adrian agreed. "It sounds like he genuinely cared about this woman too. You don't think they were romantically involved, do you?"

"No. Surprisingly, I think they actually had a platonic friendship. She mentions her husband in later letters. How much better he was doing in Arizona and that the money they'd gotten from the sale of the inn had helped pay for his medical care, and my father seems genuinely happy to hear that. There's no hint of anything untoward between them at all."

"Well, that must be a relief," Adrian said. "To know he was a little less of a bastard than you thought, I mean."

"I'm not sure." Erik frowned. "I mean, yes, it is good to know. But it doesn't change the terrible things he did. It doesn't erase the fact that he hurt my mother deeply."

"I guess it goes to show that people are far more complex than we want to acknowledge," Jay said quietly. "Bad people do good things, and good people do bad things. It's not always so easy to fit that all in a neat little box."

Adrian glanced over at Jay. He wasn't looking at Adrian at all as he said it, but his gaze flickered over to Adrian's for a brief moment. *I'm sorry I hurt you*, Adrian thought, wishing Jay could hear him. *I'd undo it if I could.*

"You're right, of course," Erik said. "And it isn't as though I have no good memories of him. He wasn't a monster with no redeeming qualities. Just a very flawed, selfish man who put his needs above that of his wife and son."

"I'm sorry." Seth rubbed his arm. "Dredging all this up can't be easy."

Erik pulled him closer. "It isn't but I'm glad I found this information. At least, the mystery has been solved, and I can feel better about the situation. It makes me very glad I decided not to sell the inn myself, though. I'd be rather surprised to find Grace is still alive, but I want to see if I can hunt down her or any of her relatives. They might find the family history interesting."

"Oh, that's a nice thought," Seth said. "I like that."

"I'm surprised your father didn't take you to the inn when you were a kid," Jay said. "If he'd had such a good time there ..."

"You know, I'm not sure he didn't," Erik said thoughtfully. "There are some pictures of my parents and me on vacation when I was quite small, and I'm standing in a courtyard of some sort. They weren't labeled so I had no idea where they were taken, and I never thought twice about them, but once I pull them out, I might be able to tell. The lamps at the inn are rather distinctive, and they're certainly old enough to have been the originals."

Seth's eyes gleamed. "Oh, please do. I would love to see more pictures of you as a kid."

Erik huffed out a little laugh. "I'll see if I can dig them up soon."

"If you want pictures of Seth, our parents have a boatload," Adrian offered.

Seth stuck his tongue out. "No one needs to see that. I was an awkward-looking kid."

"He really was," Adrian agreed.

But rather than give him shit back, a startled expression crossed Seth's face. "Oh shit, Erik, we need to get ready and head out soon."

Erik grimaced as he glanced at the clock. "You're right. We do."

"Where are you going?" Adrian asked. Seth hadn't mentioned anything to him about plans.

"Wedding planning," Seth said with a grin. "You're not invited."

"I'm heartbroken," Adrian said, clutching his chest in mock agony. "How could you do this to me, brother?"

"Oh, you'll be brokenhearted when you learn where we're going," Erik said with a little grin as he left the den.

"Where are you going?" Jay said. He sounded as curious as Adrian felt.

"We're meeting Rex Garland and his boyfriend for dinner tonight." Seth waggled his eyebrows. "Wouldn't you like to tag along?"

"Damn, I *am* a little jealous," Adrian admitted. "You're meeting with them to discuss Rex performing at your wedding, I take it?"

"Yup. It all kinda came together last minute. We were originally going to do a Skype meeting, but he realized he had a show scheduled here, and once I figured out I'd be in Philly at the same time ..." Seth shrugged. "He offered to meet in person, and I was *not* going to turn that down."

"Some people have all the luck," Jay said. Adrian glanced at him, wondering if he was upset—since his own luck hadn't exactly been stellar lately—but he had a wry little grin on his face.

"Well, what are you waiting for?" Adrian said. "Go!"

"Sorry to leave you guys," Seth said. "I meant to say something earlier, but it slipped my mind. You're welcome to anything in the kitchen, of course. Help yourselves. Or there're a ton of nearby restaurants if you don't feel like cooking."

"I can entertain myself for an evening," Adrian said with a laugh. "You don't have to look after me. Have fun on your double-date with Rex."

Seth shot him a huge grin before he disappeared out the door, presumably to get cleaned up.

"Should we break down the rest of these boxes, clean up the trash, then figure out what we want to do tonight?" Adrian asked, turning to Jay, who had been standing there with his hands in his pockets as he surveyed the disaster of a room.

He nodded. "Sounds good."

They worked quickly and quietly for the most part, but it didn't feel particularly tense. They had it nearly cleaned up by the time Erik and Seth called out their goodbyes and left.

"Well"—Adrian sat back on his heels—"what do you say we shower, then figure out our own dinners."

"Sure. You want the first shower or the second?"

No offer to share one, unfortunately, Adrian thought. But he didn't want to push his luck. "Second is fine. I'll probably give the kids a quick call first."

"You're close," Jay said. It sounded more like an observation than a question.

"We are." Adrian smiled. "I miss them a lot when they're at their mom's."

Jay nodded once, then left the room.

Well, okay then.

———

"And you were good for your mom today?" Adrian asked his kids. Jay was still in the shower, and Adrian had been chatting with them for about fifteen minutes.

"'Course!" Josh grinned at him, showing off the new gap in his teeth that had appeared since Adrian last saw him.

"Better get that tooth under the pillow, kiddo," Adrian reminded him. "Or the Tooth Fairy won't visit."

"I can't! I swallowed it! I woke up and it was gone!"

"Oh, boy," Adrian muttered under his breath.

"Right?" Michelle peeked over Josh's shoulder. "I told him to leave a note for the Tooth Fairy explaining the situation and that she might make an exception."

"Well, let's hope so," Adrian said. "But I should get going. I need to figure out dinner. Love you guys! Bye, Michelle!"

His kids echoed his love, and his ex-wife gave him a small wave. "Bye, Adrian! See you in a few days."

After he hung up, he looked around the empty loft. He and Jay had the place to themselves this evening. That was promising. Maybe he could make something for dinner for them both. He was a better baker than cook, but he could certainly throw something together that would hopefully impress Jay. He'd seemed to enjoy breakfast this morning.

Maybe after dinner, they could have a drink, talk a little ... and hopefully, the night would end with them sharing a bed again.

———

After his shower, Adrian walked into the main living area in search of Jay but stopped in his tracks when he heard voices.

One was Jay and another was a woman. Adrian looked around, confused, before he spotted Jay at the dining room table, looking down at his phone. Presumably, he had someone on speakerphone.

"But how can you leave, Ajay? Your father and I aren't getting any younger," the woman continued. Ahh, probably his mom. Adrian remembered Jay telling him his parents had moved from India for college, and Adrian could hear the lilt of it in her voice.

"I know, Mom." Jay sounded like he was trying to be patient but struggling.

Adrian knew he should leave. This was clearly a private conversation, but his feet felt glued in place. "But I need to do this for my career. I'm just not having any luck finding a place that wants me in New York."

"You should have become a dentist like your father instead of a pastry chef. You wouldn't have these problems, and there would be plenty of work for you."

"There's plenty of work for me. It's just —"

"Yes, yes, the scandal. There's no scandal in dentists' offices. Your father hasn't had one in his whole career!"

"There—" Jay sighed. "Look, that isn't the point. I'm not a dentist, and I don't want to be one. I love what I do. I just need to do it somewhere else for a while."

"But who will take care of us?"

"Manjeera and Paavvai? You do have three children, you know."

"They have families of their own. You should be looking after us."

"Are you talking back to your mother, Ajay?" A deeper man's voice chimed in, and Adrian assumed it was Jay's father. Adrian really should stop listening. He should turn around and hide in the bedroom until Jay hung up. But he couldn't seem to make himself do it.

"I'm not talking back." There was an edge to Jay's voice. "I just don't see why I'm expected to stay in New York."

"Your sisters are in New York," his father said.

"I'm not my sisters! I'm me, and however hard it's been recently, I still love my career, and if I have to do it somewhere other than New York for a while, that's what I'm going to do." He took a deep breath. "I love you and Dad, but I'm not budging."

"You're breaking your mother's heart, Ajay," his father said.

"I'm sorry," Jay choked out. "Love you. Bye." He jabbed at the phone before he dropped his head and dug his palms into his eyes.

Unable to see Jay suffer without trying to do something, Adrian walked over to him. There was a chance he'd be pissed that Adrian had been eavesdropping on his conversation, but it seemed worth the risk.

"Hey, you okay?" Adrian asked softly. He laid a hand on Jay's upper back, just resting it there. He jerked in surprise, but he didn't throw off Adrian's hand.

"Not really." Jay lifted his head, his shoulders still slumped. "How much of that did you hear?"

"Quite a bit," Adrian admitted. He rubbed his thumb in gentle circles, feeling a knot in Jay's shoulders. He pressed a little harder, and when Jay leaned into his touch, Adrian brought his other hand up, using both his thumbs to dig into the tense muscles. "I didn't mean to snoop. I just came out to find you and ..."

"They're not bad people. They're just so ... Indian. And I'm not." Jay sighed heavily. "We're never going to see eye-to-eye on a lot of things."

"Family's complicated," Adrian said. It felt like a platitude but he didn't know what else to say.

"Oh, sure." Jay let out a little snort. "Come on, I've heard more than enough from both you and Seth about how perfect the Cobb family is."

Adrian winced but he kept rubbing. "Well, my siblings and I do have a great relationship with our parents. I'll admit that. But I'm divorced, and I think I know what family conflict is like."

Jay shrugged off his hands as he stood. "You don't know what *this* is like."

"No, I don't," Adrian admitted. "But I'm willing to listen if you'll tell me. Come on, I'll make us dinner, we can sit down and have a drink, and you can talk as much or as little as you want."

Jay's expression hardened as he swiped his phone from the table, then stuffed it in his pocket. "I don't want to talk at all. Do whatever you want to do for dinner, but I'm going out."

Adrian opened his mouth, then closed it. He stood silently as Jay stalked toward the exit, only stopping long enough to put on shoes and a coat. When he closed the door behind him, the apartment was suddenly very quiet.

"Well, that didn't go the way I hoped," Adrian muttered. "Guess I might as well go figure out dinner for myself, then."

He stared at the contents of the refrigerator for a while before he admitted he'd lost all motivation to cook. A restaurant it was. He took a few minutes to turn out all the lights, gather his own coat, and then lock up behind himself.

So much for my plan, he thought as he trudged down the sidewalk in search of a restaurant.

Every step forward with Jay was countered by two back, and at this rate, they were going to end up miles apart.

Then again, that was hardly new.

EIGHT

Adrian had lost most of his appetite, and he had little motivation to hunt for a restaurant that appealed, so he stopped at the first one he ran across. Unfortunately, it was packed. People spilled into the vestibule, and Adrian had to squeeze between them to even reach the hostess' podium. "Table for one?" he shouted over the noise.

"That'll be at least a forty-five-minute wait." The hostess gestured toward the even more packed bar. "If a spot opens up there at the bar, you're welcome to grab it but ..."

"Put me on the list for a table, I guess," he said with a resigned sigh. "Last name, Cobb."

It was 7 p.m. on a Saturday night in a downtown Philly restaurant. Every other place in the area was likely as swamped, and he didn't have the motivation to drive to the outskirts of town where it might be less busy. He knew this place wasn't going to be in any hurry to seat a single person at a bigger table, though, so he resigned himself to a long wait.

He managed to squeeze himself into a small pocket of space between a straight couple, who couldn't keep their hands off each other, and a group of guys, who looked like they'd just gotten off work. He let the noise of the conversations wash over him as he pulled his phone out of his pocket and fiddled with it. He kept half an eye on the people around him to make sure he wasn't in anyone's way as he played a mindless puzzle game while he waited. But when a small group pushed past him, trying to reach the door to leave, they shoved him back, and he nearly lost his footing. A hand between his shoulder blades steadied him, and once the group was out the door, he twisted around to thank the person who had kept him from tipping over.

"Thanks, I—" He blinked as he saw Jay with an equally startled expression on his face.

"Adrian?"

"Oh, shit. Sorry." Adrian grimaced. "I swear I'm not following you. It's just …"

"The closest restaurant to Seth and Erik's apartment if you turn left," Jay finished, sounding more resigned than anything else.

"Yeah. Guess we both turned left."

Jay let out a humorless little chuckle. "Guess so."

"Look, I can go somewhere else," Adrian offered. "If you want."

"No, that would be ridiculous. We're adults. We can eat in the same restaurant."

"Thanks." Adrian offered him a tentative smile before turning away.

He'd rather talk to Jay, but he'd already pushed his luck today. No point in antagonizing him further. Adrian returned to his puzzle and tried not to obsess over the fact that the man he wanted was just a few feet away. Ignoring him.

"Table for Sun-ager!" the hostess called out, and Adrian glanced up. She'd butchered the pronunciation, but Jay squeezed past Adrian, holding up a hand to indicate he'd heard her.

The waitress smiled at Jay. "Right this way."

Jay started after her but he paused and glanced back at Adrian. "Come on. It's stupid for you to wait another half hour just to get a table. We can share."

It took Adrian a second to process Jay's offer, but Jay had already begun to weave through the crowd in the server's wake. "Oh, um, thanks," Adrian managed as he did his best to keep up with them.

The waitress gave Jay a confused look when Adrian approached the table. "I thought there was just one in your party?"

"My friend is joining me," Jay explained. "We just ran into each other, and I figured we might as well share a table."

"I was on the waitlist too," Adrian explained as he hung his coat off the back of the chair. "So you can take Cobb off there."

"Oh, great." She smiled at them both. "Let me grab a second menu."

After they'd ordered drinks and food, they stared at each other from across the small table. It was tucked up against the window, and with a small candle burning in between them, it felt cozy, like they were on a date. Except, they'd never been on a date. They'd spent a lot of time in bed before Adrian up and disappeared from Jay's life, but they'd never been on a date.

Jesus, I am an asshole. Definitely a grade-A asshole.

"So, this is awkward," Adrian said.

Jay laughed, the tense set of his shoulders softening. "It is. And I'm sorry I stormed out earlier. I shouldn't have taken everything with my parents out on you."

"No, I listened in on a private conversation, then intruded with completely unsolicited advice and sympathy. I deserved it."

"I knew you were there listening," Jay admitted. "I could have paused the conversation and told you to go elsewhere or left myself. And let's be honest ... I overreacted to your comment."

"We're both pretty on edge," Adrian acknowledged. "I've been trying to apologize for what I did last year, and you probably hate my guts for it. Which is fair. I think I've been going about this all wrong, though," he added. "I'm not trying to be pushy. I just wanted an opportunity to say I'm sorry for my shitty behavior—"

"Look, I'm not saying I'm okay with what you did last year," Jay said. "But I sort of understand it better now. You were looking for an escape from your life that weekend, and it turned into something more. Something you never anticipated."

"It did." Adrian looked down. "But I really should have told you the truth about my situation. Or, at the very least, told you I couldn't pursue something once reality hit again. You deserved a whole lot better than I gave you."

The waitress appeared with drinks and set them in front of them. "Can I get you anything else?"

After checking with Adrian, Jay politely dismissed her. When she was gone, he gave Adrian a serious look. "What happened last year wouldn't have been so bad if it hadn't happened before."

"Before?"

"You're not the first guy to ghost me."

"Oh." Adrian grimaced. "That sucks."

"It really does. And happens to a lot of my friends. Gay, straight, male, female, doesn't seem to matter. You make what you think is a connection with someone and they just disappear. It's hurtful."

"The connection between us was real," Adrian said, leaning in.

"I guess I'm in the minority then because I can't imagine just disappearing on someone I had that kind of connection with." He looked down at his hands.

"I don't have a good excuse for it," Adrian said. "I got spooked, but that doesn't justify it."

"Spooked because of the distance and the kids?"

"Partly. But Seth pointed something out the other day. It probably didn't help that I was dealing with some custody stuff. My ex hasn't been great about me being bi—"

"Yeah, I remember you saying that."

"So I think some part of me was worried she'd use it against me in court."

"Oh." The look of shock on Jay's face was genuine. "Do you think she'd do that?"

"Now? No. But then? I didn't feel like I knew her *at all* anymore. I wasn't sure what she'd do. And I was terrified of losing my kids."

"You could have told me, Adrian. I would have understood."

"I should have." He looked down at his drink. "Maybe I was a little gun shy about trusting someone new as well. I don't know. It had been a long time since I'd felt anything for anyone but

Michelle. It was probably way too soon to get into a serious rela-tionship, and there's no way what we had wouldn't have been serious."

"True."

"I'm not making excuses. I just want you to understand the reasons."

"I do." Jay took a deep breath, but anything else he might have said was cut off by the waitress arriving with their dinners.

"This looks good," Adrian said. He'd ordered the mushroom and sausage gnocchi and Jay had giant meatballs in a pool of sauce with grilled bread.

"Yeah, it does." Jay took a bite, then chewed. "I wonder where Seth and Erik were meeting Rex Garland and his husband tonight."

"I don't know. I know I'm jealous as fuck, though," Adrian admitted.

Jay let out a genuine sounding laugh. "Me too."

"I guess we'll get to meet him at the wedding, though."

"Guess so." Jay used some of the bread to mop up the sauce on the plate. "I guess we should discuss their wedding cake at some point too."

"Do you actually want to work with me on it?"

Jay looked surprised. "Yeah, why? Don't you want to work together?"

"No, I do," Adrian assured him. "I just wanted to give you an out if you wanted it. Sometimes, Seth gets ideas and he sort of steamrolls over people. I don't want this to be awkward for you."

"It's not awkward," Jay said firmly. "I'm fine with it."

"Can we clear up one thing I've been wondering about?" Adrian asked.

"Sure." But despite Jay's easy words, he looked apprehensive. "What did you want to know?"

"What was earlier about?"

"Earlier?"

Adrian dropped his voice. "The, uh, voyeurism yesterday."

"Oh." Jay rubbed the back of his neck. "I don't know. It was a weird impulse. I mostly wanted to see if you'd do it."

"Well, I did." Adrian let out a self-conscious little laugh.

"Yeah, you did." There was heat in Jay's eyes again, and when their knees bumped under the table, he didn't pull away.

————

"Do you want to grab a drink?" Jay asked after they'd settled the bill, split because neither of them would agree to let the other pay. "Somewhere else, I mean."

"Uh, sure," Adrian agreed as he shrugged on his coat. "Did you have a place in mind?"

"Maybe that bar we passed the other night on the way back from the steakhouse?"

"I didn't even *notice* a bar," Adrian admitted. He'd been too wrapped up in actually being able to have a conversation with Jay. "But sure. Lead the way."

The place Jay took them to turned out to be a dive bar with several small TVs, dartboards, and pinball machines in the back.

They took a seat at one of the available U-shaped booths, and Adrian studied the beer menu before settling on one of his favorite bottled beers.

"This is nice," he said after they had drinks in front of them. The bar had a fun vibe with art on the walls and while there was music playing, it wasn't so loud they couldn't talk. It did ensure he and Jay sat fairly close together though, which was A-okay with Adrian. They were at a ninety-degree angle to each other, and Adrian's knee pressed firmly against Jay's thigh. He had his shirtsleeves rolled up to reveal his strong forearms, and Adrian really wanted to bury his hands in Jay's thick black hair and kiss him senseless. He played with the beer bottle instead, rolling it back and forth in his palms.

"I just wanted someplace low-key where we could talk."

"What do you want to talk about?"

"Honestly, I don't know." Jay let out an annoyed sounding laugh that made Adrian smile. "I'm just tired of fighting with you."

"I don't like it either."

"So, truce?"

"Yeah, I'd like that. I can't undo what happened before, but it would be nice to be friends." Adrian snuck a quick glance at him. "But, um, I'd be lying if I said I haven't thought about you in a, uh, more than friendly way."

"I watched while you jerked off the other day, Adrian. Hell, I told you to do it. I think we can safely assume the feeling is mutual."

He shrugged. "It could have just been a way to gain some power over me."

The startled expression on Jay's face led Adrian to believe he'd never even considered that possibility. He was silent a moment. "I guess ... yeah, maybe that could have been a part of it."

Adrian wet his lips. "But not all of it?"

"No, not all of it," Jay said quietly. "Not even close."

The conversation turned in other directions as one of them commented on the basketball game showing on ESPN on the TV nearby, and they got into a friendly argument about teams. Adrian was a die-hard Penn State fan while Jay rooted for Syracuse. Adrian was able to forget that they'd ever been at odds. Right now, it felt like the intervening year had never happened, and they were just two guys who'd met and hooked up one weekend and were now out at a bar enjoying each other's company again. Adrian liked that Jay didn't shrink from their good-natured disagreement, instead, giving as good as he got as they discussed team rivalries and the upcoming March madness playoffs.

Jay grabbed Adrian's forearm at one point, probably to emphasize something he was saying, but he left his hand there, and Adrian enjoyed the warmth—even through the fabric of his shirt. The dingy bar seemed to gleam with far more luster than it probably deserved as they each ordered a second drink, and they debated which team was going to win the NCAA conference title. Adrian loved watching Jay's brown eyes light up and the way he kept sliding a little closer to Adrian so they were touching constantly.

After Jay drained his second drink, he set it on the table and glanced over at Adrian through his dark lashes. "What do you say we get out of here and head back to the loft?"

The words were innocent enough, but Adrian had seen a similar intensity in Jay's eyes before, and he knew exactly what it meant.

Was it a good idea? Probably not, but he didn't have it in him to fight the attraction between them.

"Yeah, I'm good with that," Adrian said hoarsely. He drained his beer while Jay paid their tab, and in a few minutes, they were out on the sidewalk.

The walk back to the loft was quiet, and Adrian wondered if Seth and Erik were back yet. The condo was dark and silent when they entered, though, and after Adrian hung up is his coat, he turned back to face Jay, wondering what came next and how to initiate it.

It turned out he didn't have to worry about either because Jay immediately stepped close, backing him up until he lightly bumped the apartment door. And then Jay's mouth was just inches from his own as he pressed their bodies together full-length.

"So, we're doing this?" Adrian asked a little breathlessly before Jay could lean in and kiss him.

Jay braced his hands on the door on either side of Adrian's head. "If you want."

"I do, I just—" Adrian wanted to know what this meant. Had Jay totally forgiven him? Were they going to try to start something new? But the words Adrian wanted to ask got stuck in his throat. "I do," he repeated. It was enough for now.

Jay nodded, then leaned in again to kiss him. This time, Adrian met him halfway.

Jay's mouth tasted familiar and so was the slight catch of their facial hair sliding together as they kissed. Jay tilted his head to the left, as he had before, and Adrian still had to tilt his chin down just a little. The quiet sounds Jay made when Adrian teased the seam of Jay's mouth with his tongue were the same as before.

But this time, Adrian's fingers shook as he worked the buttons loose on Jay's shirt. He licked his lips at the sight of all that smooth brown skin. He wanted to drag his tongue along that still very sexy collarbone he'd enjoyed so much in the past, but a sudden wave of apprehension washed over him, and he felt less sure of himself than he had before.

"Bedroom?" Jay said. He tugged Adrian toward it, and he felt his fears slip away with every step. His blood sang at the feel of their palms pressed together and the promise of what would happen next.

In the bedroom, with the door closed, Adrian dropped to his knees and unbuckled Jay's belt. His uncut cock felt warm and thick in Adrian's palm, maybe about half hard, and Adrian wrapped his lips around the shaft, sliding down as far as he could go. Jay's hands were gentle as he threaded them through Adrian's hair, pushing him to take his dick deeper.

They both froze at the sound of the front door opening, and Adrian heard the quiet murmur of Erik and Seth's voices. He heard the noise of footfalls near the guest room door, though he couldn't clearly hear whatever Erik said.

"Maybe they're already asleep," Seth responded. "We can talk to them in the morning."

Erik said something else that Adrian couldn't hear, and then Seth's soft laugh. "Well, maybe ..."

After the footsteps retreated, Jay cupped Adrian's cheek. "You good to keep going?"

Adrian nodded and the heat in Jay's eyes made him glad he'd said yes. And then Adrian couldn't think of anything because Jay was thrusting into his mouth, gently but insistently, and Adrian could taste his flavor on his tongue, and it was so sweet and good and familiar it made Adrian want to cry. He'd missed this, missed Jay, and he never wanted this to end. He swirled his tongue around the tip of Jay's cock, making him moan lowly. He froze at the sound. Jaye gently pulled away, and Adrian missed the connection immediately.

"Strip and bend over the bed," Jay said softly.

Adrian stood on shaky legs and removed his clothing with fingers that were still trembling. When he was naked, he turned to face the bed. Jay—who had also stripped—stepped up behind him. He pressed a warm palm to Adrian's back until he was bent over it. "Don't move."

He disappeared for a moment, and Adrian glanced over to see him pull a small pharmacy bag from his suitcase. When exactly had Jay gone out to buy condoms and lube? Adrian didn't dare ask. It didn't matter, and he needed Jay inside of him too much to question it.

Jay's fingers were warm and slick as they pushed into Adrian's body, one at a time. When they brushed Adrian's prostate, he let out an involuntary moan.

"We're going to have to be quiet."

Adrian nodded and bit his lip as Jay withdrew his fingers. After the sound of tearing foil, Adrian felt the nudge of Jay's thick cock, and Adrian really had to grit his teeth to keep from moaning. In the past year, he'd played with toys a handful of times, so it was less about the stretch than feeling Jay inside him again.

Jay let out a little sound too, a soft stuttering exhalation of breath that let Adrian know he was similarly affected.

Jay moved slowly with steady, even strokes that went deep. Adrian braced himself on the bed and held still, letting Jay grip his hips and control the pace even though he was dying for him to let loose and just fuck him deep and hard.

This was good, though. So good. Colors swam in front of Adrian's closed eyes, and he felt his cock throb when Jay nudged his prostate just right. No toy could ever feel this good. And Jay still knew just how to drive Adrian absolutely crazy.

Adrian wasn't used to being this quiet or still, though. He clenched around Jay's cock and felt his hips stutter. Adrian smiled at the reaction. There, he could make Jay lose his cool too. But Jay nudged him forward until he climbed onto the bed and knee-walked forward far enough for Jay to kneel on the bed behind him. They were still connected, and Jay pulled him back so the back of Adrian's thighs rested on the front of Jay's. Jay's body curved around his, muscles hard, skin soft and warm, and Jay placed his palm in the middle of Adrian's chest.

It felt so right like this—their bodies connected, the distance between them non-existent. Adrian was exactly where he wanted to be. Adrian let his head fall back until their cheeks brushed, and he began to move, rising and falling over Jay's cock until he felt his orgasm begin to grow, choking out all other thought.

"Close," he managed in a strangled whisper. Jay pushed him forward so his hands landed on the mattress and Jay had leverage. He fucked him hard through those last few strokes, and Adrian had to bury his head against a nearby pillow to muffle his cries. He spent all over the sheets and felt the moment when Jay came too, his hips stuttering and his hands bruising on Adrian's waist.

Jay draped himself over Adrian's back, panting hard for a moment before he straightened, then carefully slid out.

Adrian stood, feeling the tightness in his thighs and the mild ache of having someone inside him for the first time in over a year.

They cleaned up silently, each taking their turn in the bathroom, but when Adrian came out, they stood on either side of the bed, staring at each other. Adrian crawled in on one side and waited to see what Jay would do. He seemed frozen in place, staring at the tangled sheets.

"You want to sleep here?" Adrian threw back the covers. "It seems silly to bother with the air mattress if we're ..." He didn't finish his thought, unsure how to word it. What *were* they doing?

Adrian held his breath as Jay looked between the comfortable king-sized bed and the smaller and less inviting air mattress.

"Sure."

Adrian tried not to make an obvious sound of relief as Jay lifted the covers and slid into the bed next to him. They were making progress.

Weird progress but progress. It was something, right?

———

Adrian awoke in the middle of the night to Jay snoring quietly beside him. Not even a snore really, just a soft rasp to his breathing. He was facing away from Adrian so all he could see was his back. Adrian desperately wanted to reach out and touch him, but he was afraid of waking him. Afraid of what he'd be like this morning. Would he regret what they'd done last night?

Did Adrian regret what they'd done? He considered the idea. No, not really. It had been great sex. Amazing sex. Something still felt off, though, and Adrian couldn't quite put his finger on it. Was it that Jay had hesitated before getting into bed with him? Or that they'd rolled to opposite sides of the bed to sleep rather than tangling up in each other as they'd done in the past?

The moment Jay had orgasmed, he'd seemed to wall himself off, and Adrian hated it. He missed the closeness. It felt different than the last time. Then, they'd talked about their fears and dreams. How nice it was to connect to someone who understood what the other was going through.

They'd shared war stories from the kitchens they'd worked in. Compared burn marks on their hands and forearms. Swapped tales of tyrannical chefs and crazy near-disasters. There was a camaraderie there that Adrian had never felt with anyone before. But now, it was like lying in bed with a stranger.

Jay sighed and flopped onto his back. He cracked one eye open and smiled at Adrian. The smile sent a pulse of relief through Adrian, and he smiled back.

"Hey."

"Hey." Jay sounded sleepy. "What time is it?"

"Early. Way too early even for me." He nodded at the window across the room. "We forgot to close the shade."

"No wonder it's so bright in here." Jay scooted a little closer. "But since we're both awake ..."

Jay reached out to touch Adrian's chest. Adrian's breath hitched when Jay smoothed his thumb across his nipple.

Jay flipped on his side, sliding closer so he could kiss Adrian's chest. He rubbed his nose through Adrian's chest hair, then flicked his tongue over Adrian's nipple. It was hard from the chilly air of the room, and the feeling of Jay working it over with his warm lips and tongue made Adrian's head swim. He slid his fingers through Jay's silky hair, encouraging him to continue.

"Mmm." He let out a little groan when Jay bit down gently. As Jay let go and the cool air hit it, his nipple pebbled further. When

Jay switched to the other one, Adrian closed his eyes, feeling his cock harden at the attention to such a sensitive spot on his body. The tiny sting of pain from Jay's teeth only heightened it, and Adrian was about to push Jay back and do the same to him. But before he could get a chance, Jay sat back. He flipped onto his back and reached for something on the nightstand. Without another word, he held up a condom, one eyebrow cocked.

Okay, that was a clear invitation if Adrian had ever seen one. He nodded, and Jay threw back the covers to reveal his erection. *Well, all right then.*

Adrian reached for the lube as Jay rolled the condom over his cock. He didn't do more than swipe some over his hole and down the length of Jay's cock before he shifted on his knees to straddle Jay's hips. Adrian sank down with a little groan, biting his lip as he saw Jay's brow furrow with concentration. Jay's lips parted in a silent gasp as Adrian bottomed out.

Fuck that was good. This was one of the few positions they hadn't tried that weekend, and he suddenly wondered why. He settled his hands on Jay's smooth chest, then began to move.

Jay let his head fall back on the pillow, dark lashes fanned out over his cheeks as he dug his teeth into his bottom lip. Adrian stared down at the scruff on his face and the long lines of his throat. He wanted to burn this moment into his memory to take out later. A strange sense of fear settled over him as he wondered if he would see Jay again after this week was up. Once he went home to Pittsburgh, would they keep in contact or would he spend lonely nights in bed, replaying this moment, and missing Jay?

"Hey, you okay there?" Jay asked, and Adrian blinked, realizing he'd stilled completely, and Jay was staring up at him with a puzzled frown. Jay ran his hands up and down Adrian's thigh in a soothing motion.

Adrian smiled reassuringly, putting all thoughts of what happened next out of his head. He had a gorgeous man under him. That was what mattered at the moment.

"Oh, I'm very good." He leaned down and brushed his lips across Jay's. Jay met him in a hungry kiss, and he wrapped his hands around Adrian's hips. Adrian took the hint, rocking his pelvis to gently raise and lower on Jay's cock. After a while, it became too difficult to kiss, so he rested his forehead against Jay's and concentrated on the feel of Jay deep within him and the growing urge to come.

"Sit up," Jay whispered, and Adrian did, staring down at Jay as he continued to fuck himself on Jay's dick. The slow, even strokes made Adrian's toes curl with pleasure, and when Jay wrapped a hand around Adrian's dick, Adrian had to bite down hard on his lip to keep from crying out.

Jay's gaze never left his as he licked his palm and stroked Adrian. The swipe of his thumb across the head of Adrian's cock made him cry out, and Jay reached up, pressing his other hand across Adrian's mouth. "Shh," he coaxed.

Adrian nodded, but he didn't push Jay's hand away, only sped up. With every sweet slide of Jay's cock in and out of him, Adrian's need ramped up higher, and he saw Jay's abs tense as he gritted his teeth.

"I'm close," Jay whispered. He twisted his grip as he slid his hand up Adrian's cock, and Adrian felt his balls grow tight and hard.

"Me too," he managed against Jay's palm. Jay dropped his hand to Adrian's hip, thrusting up into Adrian in a way that made Adrian's eyes water. But it wasn't until Jay softly called out, "Adrian," and shuddered up into him that pleasure welled up in him, too big to contain, and he spurted across Jay's stomach, painting white across the dark trail of hair below his navel.

Jay fell back onto the pillows with a quiet groan, still gently stroking Adrian. His cock was spent for the moment, and he was almost too sensitive, but he enjoyed the shuddery little sensations Jay kept eking out of him. They both panted lightly, and Adrian leaned down to kiss Jay. He half-expected Jay to push him away, but instead, he kissed Adrian back with an intensity that Adrian hadn't felt since they'd said goodbye in New York. When Jay's hand slowed on Adrian's cock, Adrian carefully lifted off. He stripped the condom off Jay, then wrapped it in a tissue from the nightstand. Adrian settled onto his side, facing Jay, who mirrored his pose. Jay lay with his head pillowed on his bent arm, and all Adrian could do was stare for a moment. Fuck, he was gorgeous.

"Wow," Adrian managed.

Jay shot him a small smile, then yawned. "Mmhmm," he said drowsily.

"Want to get some more sleep?" Adrian asked. He wanted to reach out and smooth the hair away from Jay's ear but it felt a little too intimate, so he contented himself with draping an arm over Jay's midsection.

A soft snore was his only answer, and Adrian smiled to himself, settled his head on the pillow, and fell asleep too.

NINE

It was much later that Adrian finally awoke. Jay was awake already and doing something on his phone.

"Morning."

"Morning." Adrian wet his lips, feeling apprehensive about everything that had transpired in the past twenty-four hours.

"What's that look for?" Jay asked with a puzzled frown.

"I don't know." Adrian flipped onto his back. "I guess I'm just feeling a little weird about things."

"Stop thinking so much, Adrian," Jay said with a groan. "I can see that face of yours, and you're trying to figure out what the fuck I'm up to. I'm not up to anything, okay?"

"It's a little scary you can read me so well," Adrian said drily. "And I wouldn't blame you if you were." Adrian could see Jay looking down at him, and their gazes met and held. "I really fucked up last year."

"Yeah, you did," Jay agreed as he patted the center of Adrian's chest. "But last night and this morning were good. Let's not dwell on the past. Let's just let it go, okay?"

"I'm not sure I can. I feel so guilty. I keep thinking about all of the ways I could have handled it differently. Jesus, just a text with 'I don't think I can do this,' would have been something. Not enough but something at least."

"It would have," Jay agreed. "It would have at least removed all of the horrible scenarios going through my head where I wondered if your plane had crashed or you'd been hit by a car on the way home from the airport or ..."

Adrian covered his face with his hands. "I'm such an asshole for doing that to you." His words came out muffled.

Jay pried his hands away from his face. "Can you stop with the self-flagellation? It's pointless."

"I just want you to know how truly sorry I am."

"Hey, I know that." Jay's voice softened. "Look, when I saw you a couple days ago, yeah, I was pissed. I won't deny that. And I've been holding onto that anger for the past year, so it kinda spewed out. But what good is it doing either of us for me to stay pissed about it? It doesn't change a thing. We both know you fucked up. You admitted it. Let's just ... let it go."

"Is that what this is about then?" Adrian gestured vaguely to their bodies tangled together under the blankets.

"The sex?"

"Yeah."

"I don't know what you mean."

"Why are we having sex?"

Jay blinked at him. "Because we both enjoy it, hopefully?"

"Of course, I enjoy it," Adrian said, feeling a little exasperated. "I just mean ..."

Jay glanced over his shoulder and winced. "Look, I really hate to cut you off there, but I seriously have to get up right now and shower or I am going to be late for my interview."

"Oh, shit." Adrian sat upright. "No, go. I won't keep you."

"Thanks. We can talk more later, okay?"

"Okay." Adrian got out of bed. "You want me to drive you?"

Jay snuck a glance at the clock as he strode to the bathroom. "Could you? I was going to ask Seth to but ..."

"No, that's fine." Adrian followed him. "Actually, I need to go pick up souvenirs for the kids and some baking supplies. Today, I'm going to make some cupcakes and leverage my brother's stupid social media presence for the good of my bakery."

Jay chuckled as he turned on the water in the shower. "Sounds like a great plan."

"You mind if I hop in with you?" Adrian gestured toward the space quickly filling up with steam. "I just need to rinse off." He pointed down at the sticky cum matting his body hair. They hadn't done much to clean up after their middle of the night sex, and Adrian felt gross.

"Go for it." Jay ducked inside and Adrian followed. Adrian was in and out in under two minutes, dried off, then dressed hurriedly. It didn't matter what he looked like, but Jay would probably appreciate having the space to get ready, and Adrian could make him coffee and toast at least.

A mug of coffee and still-warm buttered toast was waiting when Jay stepped into the kitchen twenty minutes later. He stopped in his tracks. "You didn't have to do that."

Adrian shrugged, brushing his own toast crumbs from his fingertips. "I didn't mind." He gestured with his mug. "Come on. Eat up, then send me the address of where I'm taking you."

<hr>

All of Erik's paperwork had been cleared away from the kitchen island, so an hour or so later, Adrian had all of his supplies spread across the counter as he stirred the flour, baking soda, and baking powder together in a bowl with a pinch of salt.

"Oooh, what are you making?" Seth peered over his shoulder. Adrian started; he hadn't heard his brother come in.

"Cupcakes."

Seth flicked his bicep with his finger. "I figured that much out from the muffin tins, liners, and fancy pastry bag. None of which Erik or I own. Did you seriously go to a baking supply store this morning?"

"Yes."

"You are terrible at vacations."

Adrian shrugged. "As long as I don't have to do it en mass or on a deadline, baking never feels like work. It's relaxing."

"So what flavor?" Seth picked up a spice jar. "Cardamom?" He inspected the bottle of rosewater on the counter next and wrinkled his nose. "Rose? Isn't that going to taste like soap?"

"Not if I do it right." Adrian dumped the finely chopped pistachios into the bowl.

"And pistachios?"

"You really don't have any faith in me, do you?" He turned to face his brother. "It's a pistachio olive oil cupcake base. The little bit of salt and nuttiness will help balance out the sweet floral of the frosting."

"If you say so." Seth still sounded skeptical, but he stepped back and gestured at the other side of the kitchen island where his laptop sat. "Can I hang out here while you bake? I have some work to do so I won't bug you while you cook, I promise."

"Sure." Adrian shook some more shelled pistachios into a bowl, then slid the package toward Seth. "I know you just want these anyway."

Seth shot him a vaguely guilty look.

"It's fine," Adrian said with a laugh. "Seriously. I bought extra because I knew you'd want them."

Seth's grin lit up his face. "Thanks. You're a pretty good brother, you know that?"

"I just moved you into your boyfriend's apartment, and now I'm baking cupcakes for you. I'm a damn good brother, you asshole."

Seth stuck out his tongue. "Hey, did Jay get off to his interview okay?"

"Yep, he's there now. I drove him in this morning."

"Oh. Good."

Adrian gave his brother a puzzled look. "Where's your better half, by the way? He doesn't strike me as the sleep-in late type."

"He left while you were out. He has plans with his daughter, Joanna. He asked if I thought he should cancel, but they don't get a ton of time together, so I told to him to go for it. I didn't figure you'd mind if it was just the two of us this morning."

"I dunno," Adrian said drily. "You are a pain in the ass to put up with. It's nice to have a buffer."

Seth shot him the finger, then cleared his throat. "So what did you and Jay get up to last night?"

Adrian measured out the olive oil as he thought of the taste of Jay's cock on his tongue. "We had dinner at the Italian place nearby, then grabbed a couple of drinks at some dive bar."

"Sounds like a nice date."

Adrian cracked eggs into a bowl, then glanced up at his brother. "It wasn't a date."

"You sure about that?"

"No. Maybe. I don't know." Adrian shrugged as he whisked the eggs, olive oil, and honey together. "Whatever it was, it was nice. We cleared the air about a few things."

"That's good." Seth cracked open a pistachio. "I thought about knocking on your door, but I wasn't sure if you guys were still up when we got home."

"Yeah, I heard you get back, but I was pretty ready to get in bed." Not to sleep but ...

Seth raised an eyebrow as if he could tell exactly what Adrian meant by that.

"So, how was your double date with Rex Garland and his husband?" Adrian asked, knowing it would distract Seth.

"Amazing," Seth gushed. "Rex is just ... wow. And his husband is a sweetheart. Total bear. They are adorable together."

Adrian snickered. "Sounds like someone has a crush."

"You would too if you'd been there."

"Probably," Adrian agreed. He didn't follow celebrity gossip much, but even he had been sucked into their love story. Then again, it wasn't often there was news about gay couples, much less a famous singer falling in love with an ordinary guy. Their story had been so sweet and wholesome too. "So they're all set to sing at your wedding?"

"Yup." Seth cracked open another nut, then dropped the shell onto the little pile beside him. "We just finalized details and discussed logistics of how the press and fans will be dealt with."

Adrian made a face as he scooped the batter into the muffin tin liners. "That sounds like kind of a nightmare to me."

"I can handle it for one day. Honestly, I know I'll be so wrapped up in Erik I won't really notice all the behind the scenes stuff, and if it'll help the inn get a little publicity ..." He shrugged.

"If Jay and I make the cake for your wedding, maybe I can leverage a little publicity for the bakery too."

"If we do a good enough job on the cupcakes today, you won't need the publicity later this summer," Seth said. "Though, it can't hurt to have extra."

Adrian slid the cupcakes into the preheated oven, then set a timer.

"So, how'd you come up with this pistachio rose cupcake idea anyway?"

"It just came to me a while back." Adrian busied himself with cleaning up the mess on the counter and loading the dishwasher. "I was thinking about the fact that our family has some Greek and Italian heritage. And, of course, Cobb is English." Adrian shrugged. "I thought about incorporating some flavors from those regions into something to sell at the bakery."

"That's a neat idea," Seth said.

"I made a couple batches that were okay but nothing spectacular. There was still something missing."

"The cardamom?"

"Yep. That was Jay's suggestion."

"Oh." Seth sounded surprised. "How did that come about?"

"It happened at the baking expo."

Adrian and Jay finally dragged themselves out of bed and downstairs to one of the demonstrations. They'd missed the bread and cake decorating competitions so far. Adrian didn't care. Being in bed with Jay was far more important. This was interesting, though.

"I like that piping technique," Adrian said quietly. They were seated toward the back of the room, but thanks to a camera feed and a big TV display, he could see the person at the front demonstrating how to pipe buttercream in a two-toned rose pattern. Not that he hadn't learned about ten thousand other piping techniques already, but this was unique. Too frilly for most cakes but great for things like Mother's Day or weddings.

"Yeah me too. Although, I don't know how often I'd use it," Jay said.

"Might work for the cupcakes I'm creating, actually. Although, I seem to be stuck in the flavor development."

"Yeah? What have you come up with so far?"

"Olive oil and pistachio cupcakes. With a hint of rosewater in the buttercream." He explained the tie-ins to his family heritage.

"Yum. And I like the sentiment."

"I feel like I'm missing something, though. It needs another component."

"Hmm." Jay seemed to be mulling the idea over. "What about something like cardamom? It would add that nice warm note to balance out the lighter flavors of the rose and pistachio. That's more my heritage than yours but ..."

"No, that sounds great." Adrian quickly warmed to the idea. "That little bit of warm spice would help ground it."

"You're really gone for him, aren't you?" Seth said, snapping Adrian out of the trance he'd been in. "Jay, I mean."

"Yeah," Adrian admitted, swallowing hard. "I guess I am."

He had no idea if it would do him any good, though. Things were too precarious with Jay to be sure of anything.

———

An hour later, a line of frosted cupcakes marched across the marble counter. Adrian had skipped the rose piping technique he'd learned about last year in favor of something simpler and topped them with a sugared rose petal and a sprinkle of chopped pistachios instead. He surveyed them with a sense of satisfaction. He'd nailed both the style and flavor. He and Seth had split one earlier, and the noises Seth had made were something Adrian never, ever wanted to hear come from his brother again.

"I like the look of the cupcakes on here." Seth tapped the white stone surface. "Great contrast and just enough visual detail to add interest without distracting from them. Cararra marble is totally in right now too."

"I'll take your word for it," Adrian said, amused. He wouldn't mind a big marble slab for rolling out pastry dough because it was cold and helped keep the butter in the dough from melting too quickly, but otherwise, he couldn't get too excited about countertop materials. He was perfectly happy with the stainless steel surfaces in his bakery. Easy to clean and hygienic was good enough for him.

"Lord, you're hopeless," Seth said with a laugh. "But, we'll get you there. Okay, let me go grab my gear and we'll get this shoot underway. I have a couple ideas for styling it."

Adrian chuckled to himself at the idea of having a photoshoot for cupcakes, but his brother was the expert on this, so he'd have to trust him.

The sound of the door opening made Adrian look up. A moment later, Jay walked into the kitchen.

"How'd it go?" Adrian asked as Jay set down his portfolio.

"Really well." Jay looked pleased, and his body language was relaxed and easy. "I like the executive chef a lot. He did say there were a couple other good candidates they were considering, but at least, I'm in the running."

"That's great!" Adrian gave him an encouraging smile. "I hope one of these works out for you."

"Me too." Jay surveyed the counter in front of him, then whistled lowly. "Wow. You've been busy."

"Yep, we're about to do a photoshoot."

"Fun." Jay carefully picked up a cupcake and inspected it. "Pistachio and rosewater?"

"Yeah. With cardamom. Like we talked about." Adrian held his breath, wondering how Jay would react.

"I remember." Jay's voice was soft and so was the smile that crossed his face. They were still staring at each other when Seth walked back in the kitchen. Adrian glanced over to see him carrying a camera bag and tripod.

"Oh, Jay. How'd the interview go?"

"Great. I'll let you know when I hear more."

"Awesome." He glanced at the cupcake in Jay's hand. "Put that one down."

Jay's eyes widened, and he carefully set the cupcake on the counter. "Sorry."

"No, didn't mean to snap at you. I just want to make sure we save all the perfect ones. Seth slid a different one toward Jay. "Take that one. The frosting is a little wonky."

Adrian scowled at him.

"I just want them to look perfect in the photo," Seth said, sounding a little defensive. "We want everyone to see how good they're going to taste. And seriously, these are the best cupcakes I've ever eaten."

"High praise," Jay said with a smile as he peeled back the paper liner.

"Trust me. They earned it."

Seth fussed with the cupcakes that were still on the counter, arranging them just so. "Okay, I'm going to take a few test shots." He twisted a lens into his camera body, then took off the lens cap.

Adrian tuned his brother out as he watched Jay take his first bite of the cupcake. His eyes half-closed as he chewed, and he made a small appreciative noise.

"Oh. Adrian .... wow." Jay looked at him.

"Okay, I think I want to get some overhead shots. Let me grab the step stool. Oh, and I think I can get to my reflector ..." Seth muttered as he left the kitchen.

But all Adrian could focus on was the trail of moisture Jay's tongue left on his bottom lip as he licked the remnants of frosting away.

"Holy shit, Adrian, this is so good." Jay's voice was a low rumble of appreciation. The sound did something to Adrian.

"Yeah?"

Jay licked his lips again. "You used honey in the cupcakes, didn't you?"

Adrian nodded.

"The balance is perfect. You nailed this flavor. I'm impressed." He took another bite and closed his eyes, letting out another little sound of appreciation.

"It was half you," Adrian protested as Jay popped the last bite into his mouth. "So, at most, it was a good collaboration."

"I can think of another collaboration I'd like to do right now." Jay licked his fingers as he stepped closer. "One where I smear this frosting on your skin, then lick it off."

Adrian shuddered. "You have no idea what kind of mental image that just conjured up."

"Oh, I think I have a pretty good idea." Jay's eyes gleamed. He was so close Adrian could smell the hint of flowers and spice on his breath.

"Maybe I'll make up an extra batch of the frosting, then," Adrian said breathlessly. "I'd love to taste it on you too."

"Mmm." Jay grabbed his hips, pulling Adrian hard against him. "I like that thought even better."

As if drawn together like magnets, their lips touched. It was only chaste for a moment before Jay slid his tongue between Adrian's lips, and Adrian splayed his palm out on Jay's back. He closed his eyes as Jay gripped his hips hard, pulling them closer together. He moaned against Jay's mouth. The hint of frosting added a hint of delicious richness as Adrian deepened the kiss. Jay slotted his thigh between Adrian's legs, pressing against his cock in a way that made him harden in his jeans. Adrian slid a hand into Jay's hair, enjoying the silky texture between his fingers as he pulled their bodies even tighter together.

"Fuck, Adrian," Jay rasped as he pulled back. He dipped his head, pressing his lips against Adrian's jaw.

"Don't stop." Adrian pulled Jay in again, kissing him deeply, feeling like he could never get enough of Jay. He wanted the kiss to go on and on. He wanted to—

"Holy shit. Well, I guess you two made up." Seth snickered.

The sound of his brother's voice made Adrian spring away, and Jay did the same. Jay cleared his throat, and Adrian wiped his mouth on his hoodie sleeve.

"I can finish photographing the cupcakes while you two disappear to the guest room, if you want." Seth sounded amused. "Just keep it down in there. I definitely don't want to hear it." He made a grossed-out face.

"No, I'm good," Adrian said. He definitely, definitely had lost his erection with his brother's arrival. "What do you need me to do to help with the photos?"

Seth's gaze flicked between Adrian and Jay for a second before he said, "You can hold this reflector. It'll bounce light back onto the cupcakes to keep the light from looking too harsh."

"Right." Adrian stepped forward and grabbed it.

Jay seemed frozen in place. He had his hands jammed in his pockets and his head hung low.

"Wait, I forgot the stepladder," Seth said. "Think you two can keep it in your pants while I'm gone?"

Adrian groaned. "We are never going to live this down, are we?"

"Nope," Seth called back over his shoulder as he walked away.

"Are you okay?" Adrian said under his breath as Seth disappeared around the corner.

Jay finally lifted his head. "That probably shouldn't have happened."

"Yeah, well, we can't exactly undo it," Adrian joked. "I'm afraid my brother knows now and will harass us about it. That's just what brothers do."

"I'll take your word for it." Jay cleared his throat. "Look, I need to go check my email to make sure I haven't heard back from any of the places I interviewed with."

"Sure," Adrian said, feeling a little confused as Jay practically bolted from the kitchen. "Do what you need to do."

Seth reappeared a moment later. He looked around. "Where's Jay?"

"He had to check some emails." *And confuse the shit out of me,* Adrian mentally added.

"Just as well, he's distracting for you."

"Tell me about it," Adrian muttered. "Okay, show me what to do for these photos."

They spent another half hour shooting them from every angle and swapping out props like wooden spoons and dishtowels. It seemed excessive to Adrian, but what did he know?

After they were done, Seth set his laptop on the counter, then hooked his camera up to it to upload the images. When they were on the hard drive, Seth waved him over. "Come take a look."

Adrian peered over Seth's shoulder and watched as he clicked through the photos. "Holy shit, Seth. These look incredible."

"They're still raw. I'll tweak the levels to optimize them all, but yeah, I'm pleased with the way they turned out."

"They look so professional."

Seth reached back and smacked his thigh. "They are professional, asshole. I'm a fucking photojournalist."

"I know. I'm sorry. That didn't come out right. I'm just blown away by how amazing they look. When I think about the product photos I have on my website ..." He cringed.

"Let me take a look." Seth clicked on the browser and brought up Adrian's bakery page. He clicked through a few tabs on the page before he cringed too. "Yeah, these are awful."

"Thanks. They're the best I could do when I opened the bakery," Adrian muttered. "Michelle offered to take them, and she did a good job with the kids' pictures, so I thought why not? But even I know they're pretty crappy. Especially when I compare them to your stuff."

Seth rubbed his forehead. "For an amateur, she does a great job with pictures of Molly and Josh, but that doesn't mean she has the skill for product photography. That's a whole different ball game."

"I'm starting to see that."

"If I didn't have so much on my plate right now, I'd offer to come to Pittsburgh and update everything for you but ..."

"No, it's okay. You need to get settled here and just enjoy your time with Erik. I get that."

"Not to mention all the travel I have scheduled. And the wedding planning." He groaned.

"Hey, can you let me know the date for that? I assume I'm invited, and I'll need to take some time off at the bakery. I need as much notice as possible."

"Of course, you're invited," Seth said with a laugh. "Actually, I wanted to ask you to be my best man."

"Really?" Adrian was a little surprised. "You aren't going to ask Mitchell? Or have Sarah be your best person?" He wouldn't have been offended if Seth had picked their older brother or his twin sister instead.

"Nah. Mitchell and I are close but I feel like you and I have gotten closer lately. He won't be mad. And I was going to ask Sarah to officiate, actually."

"Really?"

"I mean, she is a minister at a Unitarian Church. It seemed like the logical thing to do. Neither Erik nor I are religious, and we're getting married at an inn so ..."

"No, that makes sense." Adrian smiled at him. "I'm flattered, man. Really. I'd be happy to."

"Jay will be a groomsman too. I was afraid that might be awkward, but based on what I saw earlier ..." Seth raised an eyebrow. "I'm thinking maybe that won't be a problem."

"Honestly, I'm not sure what's going on there," Adrian admitted. "He was so pissed, and then all of sudden we're ..."

"Fucking?" Seth supplied. "Much as it pains me to think about my brother and my roommate doing anything together, it's fairly obvious what's going on."

"Uh, yeah." Adrian dragged a hand through his hair. "I'm just really confused about what it all means."

"Only one way to find out."

"What's that?"

"Ask him." Seth gave him a pointed look. "I mean, you fucked up before by not communicating. How about you don't do that all over again, dummy."

Adrian shoved him. "When did you become the relationship guru?"

"When I clearly got better at them than you."

"Ouch." Adrian clutched his chest. "Harsh, dude. That's harsh."

"I'm just saying ..."

"Yeah, yeah," Adrian grumbled. "All right, now that I've agreed to be your best man, and you've told me how to fix my love life, what should I do about my webpage?"

"Well," Seth said slowly as he scrolled through it. "The page itself isn't bad. It's a clean, simple design, and it looks good. It's really just the photography that's a little sub-par. I think if you hired a good photographer to update all of it, that would do the trick."

"What would that run me?"

Seth shrugged. "I honestly have no idea. New York prices aren't the same as Pittsburgh, but it's worth splashing out for a professional photographer. Think of it as an investment."

"Ballpark?"

Seth named a price that made Adrian wince. "Ouch. That's a lot. But okay. I trust you on this."

"It'll be worth it," Seth assured him. "We should also talk about your social media presence at some point if you really want to improve your visibility."

"I know." Adrian rubbed his forehead. "I just have no idea what I'm doing."

"Look, Instagram is probably your best bet for marketing. I'll get you started by coming up with a list of hashtags to use. You could easily do a daily post of something in the shop. It wouldn't be too difficult to keep up with."

"My photography sucks way worse than Michelle's, and all I have is my phone camera."

"I have an idea." Seth stood. "Come on. We'll do some practice shots, and I'll show you how to use filters and adjust the lighting on Instagram. You don't need Photoshop or anything. For posts like that, the built-in filters will be plenty. You might want to invest in a ring light too."

"How much will that run me?"

"Oh." Seth laughed. "Five or ten bucks. It's just a simple light that clips onto your phone. It'll be a huge help for the product lighting, and it doesn't leave any harsh shadows."

"All right," Adrian said doubtfully as he followed Seth over to where the cupcakes were still set up on the coffee table. "I'm trusting you on this."

"Hey, who has over three hundred thousand followers?"

"You do," Adrian muttered.

"Then trust that I know what the hell I'm doing."

Half an hour later, Adrian had to admit Seth definitely *did* know what he was talking about. The photos Adrian took of his cupcakes with his phone were far better than anything he had ever taken before, and the quick editing lesson had made them look a hell of a lot more professional.

"Am I right or am I right?" Seth said smugly.

"You're right."

"I'll do some research and see if I can find some local influencers for you too. If you get the right people to pay attention to your stuff, that could really give the business a big boost. Just think about the cronut trend."

Adrian chuckled. He'd tried the cross between a croissant and a doughnut when he'd visited Seth in New York a few years ago. They were good, but they hadn't quite warranted the amount of media hype they'd been given. Still, Seth's point was well made.

"Yeah, I hear you. I'm just not used to thinking like that," Adrian admitted. "It's a whole new ball game for me.

"I know, but it won't take much. A few tweaks to what you're doing could really make a huge difference."

"I know. And I do feel like this is the next big step I need to take. I appreciate your help a lot," Adrian said as he hugged his brother. "I know I give you shit but ..."

"That's what brothers are for." Seth squeezed him tighter. "Right?"

"Right."

"And, hey, maybe if things keep going well for you and Jay, there will be another wedding in the future."

Adrian rolled his eyes. "Whoa. Don't get ahead of yourself there. Jay and I are having sex. I don't know if there's a chance for anything else." But it was impossible to deny the leap in his heart at the thought that maybe it could be more. Would Jay really have pursued anything if he didn't want to rekindle what they'd had before? Maybe this time they could do it right. The happiness that thought brought Adrian told him he needed to make it happen.

He wasn't over Jay, so why would he try to pretend he was? He just had to prove to Jay that this time, they could make this work.

TEN

The final day in Philly arrived with Adrian feeling no closer to knowing where things stood between him and Jay and what the plan for the future was. After Seth found them kissing yesterday, Jay had been quiet all evening. They'd had sex last night, and again this morning, and even now, Adrian felt a flash of heat at the thought of how it had felt when Jay slid into him from behind. Adrian still had teeth marks in his shoulder from Jay's attempt to muffle his shout.

But they hadn't talked.

Every time Adrian had made an attempt to, Jay had sidestepped it and found an excuse to leave the room. And now, it was mid-morning. Adrian had a five-hour drive ahead of him, and soon, Jay would leave for the station to take the train from Philadelphia to New York City.

Adrian had no idea what to do about Jay, and he was running out of time.

He and Seth and Jay had been lingering at the dining room table though breakfast was long over. They'd said goodbye to Erik this morning before he left for work.

"I should head out," Adrian finally said with a sigh as he stood and picked up his coffee cup. "Valentine's Day is in a week, and I have to be sure everything's ready. It's one of our biggest sales days of the year."

"I don't miss that," Jay said as he cleared their plates. "Four hundred crème brûlées and at least as many chocolate tortes."

"Tell me about it. Although, it's mostly cupcakes for me. So many damn cupcakes."

"Oh, thanks for the reminder. I keep forgetting to post those pictures I took yesterday," Seth said.

Adrian rolled his eyes. "Why am I not surprised?"

"I'll get to it this week," Seth protested as he loaded plates in the dishwasher. "Or you can make me more before you leave." He gave Adrian a cheeky grin.

"That's all the cupcakes you're getting from me for now." Adrian pointed at him. "Come to Pittsburgh if you want more."

"Oh, fine. I guess I could do that."

"I'll get my stuff together now, I guess." Adrian hesitated, feeling a lot more reluctant to leave than he'd expected. Part of it was because he hadn't realized until this week how much he'd missed spending time with his brother. But a lot of it had to do with Jay. He glanced over at him. "Hey, Jay, do you think you could help me with something?"

He looked up from where he'd been staring down at his phone, surprise written all over his face. "Uh, sure."

Adrian was glad Jay didn't ask why because he wasn't sure he could come up with a good answer on the spot.

Jay followed him into the guest bedroom, and Adrian closed the door behind them. Adrian stepped toward Jay and slid his arms around his waist. Jay pulled him closer, but a little furrow appeared between his eyebrows.

"What did you need help with?"

"Well, I wanted to talk to you about what we do now," Adrian said quietly. "We've been putting it off, but we really need to talk about this."

"What do you mean?" Jay looked even more puzzled.

"I mean ... how are we going to make this work? We didn't really talk about logistics last time, which was part of the problem. We should discuss it now, right? Do you think you could make it to Pittsburgh sometime in the near future? I can try to squeeze in a quick trip to New York soon, but I've gotta give everyone a lot of notice and——"

"Wait, Adrian. I think maybe you misunderstood something. You didn't really think this thing would go beyond this weekend, did you?" Jay looked surprised.

"You don't want this to continue?" Adrian's heart dropped to his toes.

"You do?"

"Well, yeah. I mean, it seems like we have some pretty amazing chemistry and ..." He squeezed Jay tighter, desperately hoping he could convince Jay to change his mind. "There's more to it than that, though. You're an incredible guy, and I really want to see where we can go with this."

"But you can't leave Pittsburgh."

"No, not permanently. But you're already planning to leave New York."

"Yeah, for Philly." Jay frowned. "That's still five hours between us, and I don't even have a driver's license."

"Well, I had an idea."

"An idea about what?"

"How to make it all work. Look, I know this guy who works for Le Cordon Bleu Institute in Pittsburgh. He's got an in at all the major restaurants in the area. If someone's looking for a pastry chef, he'll know about it." Adrian beamed at him.

"You want me to *move* to Pittsburgh?"

"Well, why not? You said you were done with the restaurant scene in New York. You might get a job here in Philly, but nothing's been offered yet. Why not give Pittsburgh a try?"

"Because I'm not moving for some guy," Jay snapped. "Some guy I don't even know if I can trust. Look, what we've had was great, but a couple of weekends together aren't exactly a great basis for a relationship."

"But ..." Adrian's brain felt numb like it had been shot full of Novocain, and he struggled to catch up with the direction Jay had gone. He'd been so sure he had the perfect solution and now ...

Jay cupped Adrian's face in his large hands. "Look, we've had a great time this week. You apologized for what happened last time. Let's just let this be the end of it. It'll be a good memory to look back on."

Adrian's heart dropped to the pit of his stomach. "So, what? The past few days you were using me for sex, and now you're just ... done with me?"

"That wasn't how I meant it, but I guess you could look at that way, if you want to." Jay scowled.

"Well, it's either that or ... wait, was this *payback?*"

Jay looked surprised. "What?"

"Making me feel like you were interested in me, then dropping me to pay me back for the way I fucked up before."

Jay stepped back and crossed his arms over his chest. "No. I *definitely* didn't intend it that way."

An ache formed in Adrian's chest. "It sure as hell feels like it. Like some kind of revenge for what happened last year."

Jay's expression hardened. "Well, you're the one who made me question if I could trust you, so maybe that's your guilty conscience talking. But, no, it wasn't revenge for me."

"Then what was it?"

"It was a ... an honest re-connection for a few days. But that's all it was. It wasn't the start of something new. That ship has sailed, Adrian. You have your bakery and your kids in Pittsburgh, and I know they come first. Whether I'm in New York or Philly, it doesn't change anything. You don't want a long-distance relationship, and you've made that abundantly clear."

"I ... it would be difficult for me," Adrian admitted. "But I'd try. I really would. As long as I knew there was an endpoint, I could handle it for a while. We could figure out a plan for you to come to Pittsburgh. Together."

But Jay shook his head. "No, Adrian. That's where the trust issue comes into play," he said softly. "Because I *don't* know that I believe that. Even if you swore up and down that you wanted me, I wouldn't be sure of it. I'm not uprooting my entire life for someone I'm not sure I can trust. A few days of great sex aren't enough, Adrian. How do I know I won't get to Pittsburgh and you'll change your mind?"

"I won't change my mind," Adrian argued.

"You did once."

Adrian stared at him a long moment as all hope crumbled. He wanted to argue with Jay, but it was true. He had. And while he knew there were a lot of things in his life he'd regret, screwing up this shot at a life with Jay was at the top of the list.

"What can I do to prove to you that you can trust me?" Adrian pleaded.

"There's nothing you can do." An expression of sadness crossed Jay's face as he reached out to touch Adrian's face. Adrian wanted to shake it off, but he still cared for Jay too much to be the one to reject him in any way. "It's over, Adrian." He brushed his thumb across Adrian's cheek before he stepped back with a regretful little smile.

"Right, okay." Adrian cleared his throat before his emotions became so overwhelming he did something stupid like cry in front of Jay. "Well, if you change your mind, you know how to find me," Adrian said.

Jay nodded, but Adrian didn't think for a minute he had any intention of doing that. And they'd still need to get through Seth's wedding this summer. Great. That would be fun. Adrian sighed. Good thing he had six months to go before he'd have to deal with that. Maybe the sting would fade by then, but he doubted it.

Adrian disappeared into the bathroom to grab his toiletries, then stuffed his belongings in his bag with shaking hands. Jay was packing too, though neither of them made eye-contact with each other. After Adrian zipped his bag shut, he turned to go. "Bye, Jay," he choked out.

"Bye, Adrian."

Adrian turned on his heel and left the bedroom, his heart breaking. He found Seth in the kitchen, working on his laptop at the island.

"Well, I'm outta here." Adrian smiled tightly at his brother. "Congrats on the engagement and moving in with Erik. And thanks for the cupcake shoot."

Seth cocked his head at him. "You're welcome. You okay, though? You seem …"

"Yeah, just getting anxious about getting back to the kids," he lied. "I want to get on the road so I don't hit rush hour going into Pittsburgh. You know how crazy the traffic gets."

"Yeah. Okay. I'll walk you out then."

The whole way downstairs and across the parking lot, Adrian felt Seth's gaze on him, but he couldn't look his brother in the eye without falling apart. His eyes burned and his throat felt tight as they approached his truck.

"What the fuck is going on?" Seth said. Although the words were harsh, his tone was very soft.

Adrian stared at his warped reflection in the shiny silver surface of the driver's side door. "Apparently, the thing Jay and I were doing the past few days was just a way to blow off some steam for him or something. He's not interested in more."

"Shit."

"I feel like a fucking idiot. I thought we were actually going to start over, but no. He said we should just leave it as is." His tone came out way more bitter than he'd intended. Seth rested his hand on Adrian's arm.

"I'm sorry." Seth hesitated. "Do you think maybe it's …"

"Payback?" Adrian supplied. "That's what I thought at first too, but he swears it's not. He said he just doesn't trust that I won't change my mind, and well, I can't exactly blame him. Why *should* he trust me?"

"Oh, man." Seth squeezed his arm.

"Yeah. So that sucks." Adrian swallowed hard.

"I wish I had some great advice for you. I really thought this might work out."

"Guess not." Adrian turned to look at Seth and gave him a tight smile. "But there's nothing I can do to fix it at this point, so I guess I'll just head back to Pittsburgh and try to move on. I won't make things awkward at your wedding. I promise."

"I wasn't worried about *that*." Seth hugged him. "I just feel like I'm at fault here somehow."

"How is this your fault?" Adrian finally looked his brother in the eye. "You didn't *do* anything other than happen to know both of us. This isn't on you, Seth."

"I just want you both to be happy."

"I know. And I'm sure Jay and I will be. It just isn't going to be together, I guess."

"I'm sorry."

"Yeah, me too." Adrian sighed. "But I did mean it. I do have to get out of here soon. The kids are expecting me back, and I really *have* missed them."

"Of course. Tell them Uncle Seth loves them."

"I will."

With another hug, Seth let him go. Adrian went through his usual routine of starting his truck and putting the address in his GPS. When he looked up, his brother was gone.

Adrian hit the side of his fist against the steering wheel and closed his eyes tightly as he let the disappointment hit him fully. Damn it. He'd lost Jay. Again.

He sat there for a while before a notification on his phone reminded him he needed to get going.

Adrian felt sick to his stomach as he put his truck in drive, then pulled away from the loft.

Pittsburgh, Pennsylvania

The five-hour drive from Philly to Pittsburgh was mind and butt-numbing despite several stops at rest areas along the turnpike. He was tired and grateful to be nearly home when he pulled into the driveway of his old house. It was Michelle and the kids' place now.

Adrian walked up the steps to the white colonial. It was a pretty little house. He'd been proud of it when they'd bought it, but it had been the right decision for Michelle to keep it. It gave the kids some continuity, and Adrian had been able to find a place nearby that suited his needs.

Adrian knocked on the glass of the front door, and a moment later, there was a blast of excited shouting as the door flung open. Michelle had offered to keep Molly and Josh for another night, but he'd never been happier to see their faces.

"Daddy!" Molly squealed and launched herself at him. "I missed you!"

"I missed you too!" He pressed a flurry of kisses to her face. "Lots and lots."

He felt a tug on his jeans. "Did you miss me?"

"I did!" He bent down to scoop up Josh, almost falling over at the combined weight of them. "Ooof. You guys are getting so big. I don't know how much longer I can do this."

Michelle laughed, and he looked up to see her standing in the doorway. She was still so pretty with her shoulder-length brown hair and bright blue eyes, even prettier than when they'd started dating in college. But his whole body didn't go up in flames at the sight of her soft lips or curves anymore. That fire had long since died down and been banked. It was just the comfortable glow of friendship now. It felt good. Though, it made him realize, again, how much he missed having someone in his life who was more than a friend. He'd come so close with Jay and fucked it all up before it had ever really had a chance. God, he was stupid.

"I don't know how you do it at all," Michelle said. "I can barely carry one of them at a time anymore."

"It's all that kneading of dough at the bakery," he joked. "Arms of steel."

She rolled her eyes. "Only you could work around all those sweet things every day and get *fitter*."

In the past, he might have seen it as an insult. A dig at him. But not anymore. He was glad she could tease him a little.

"Guess it's my superpower," he joked back. He glanced back at Molly and Josh. "You guys ready to go?"

"Yup! Mommy had us pack when you sent her a message saying you were close."

"Perfect." He lowered them down with a groan. For all his bragging about his superhero powers, his arms and back were very sore from holding two kids who were growing much faster than he'd like. Forget helping his brother move or going back to the gym, he should probably just start bench-pressing his children.

"Hey, can you guys get in the truck? I have a quick question for your mom before I go," he said.

"Okay!" Molly took off like a shot—if that girl didn't become a runner, it was going to be a waste because she seemed to only have one speed and it was *fast*—and Josh followed a little more slowly. Adrian smiled as Molly helped him up into the truck. She was also a very good big sister. It made him proud.

When the truck door shut behind them, Adrian turned back to Michelle, who gave him a puzzled frown. "What's going on, Adrian?"

He held up his hands. "Nothing serious. I promise. More of a hypothetical question."

"You don't want to move the kids to Philly or something, do you?" she asked, and he blinked at her.

"What? No. What would make you think that?"

She shrugged. "You just got back from there, and you looked so serious, and you didn't want the kids to overhear ..."

"No, no, it's nothing like that," he assured her. "I have no intention of leaving Pittsburgh or messing with our custody agreement or anything like that. I was just wondering something ..."

"Well, spit it out," she said, but she sounded more amused than anything else.

He stuck his hands in his pockets. "How would you feel about me dating a man?"

She blinked at him a moment. "Uhh, what?"

"I know you were always kind of uncomfortable with the idea of me being bi, and I wondered how you'd feel about it if I were dating a man."

"Have you met someone?"

"No." He sighed. "Sort of. Not really. I reconnected with someone I'd met a while back, and it got me thinking."

"Adrian, was this someone you ... were with when we were married?"

His eyes widened. "Oh, God, no. I *never* cheated on you, Michelle. We were separated by the time I met him. Divorce paperwork was filed and everything."

"Oh." The tension in her shoulders softened. "I didn't mean to accuse you of anything really. I just ..."

"No, I can see how that might have sounded."

"So you're seeing this guy now?" she prompted.

"No. Um, actually the distance is a big issue, and there's some other stuff ..." He shrugged. Way too much for him to get into with his ex-wife. "Anyway, I'm not seeing him. But it got me wondering how you'd feel if I *were* seeing a man. I haven't really dated much since we split—women or men—and I was curious. You don't have to answer, though, if you don't want to."

"It's okay." She pushed her hair off her forehead. "Um, it would be a little weird—I'm not going to lie. But I'm not sure if it's just the idea of you being with, well, someone other than me." She held up her hand as if to stop him, although he hadn't so much as opened his mouth. "Which is hugely hypocritical since I'm dating Shane but ..."

"No, I get that," he said. "The guy thing would be okay? You'd feel comfortable with the kids being around him and all that?"

"I mean, I trust you wouldn't bring anyone sketchy around our kids. So, no, it wouldn't make a difference to me if it were a man." She looked puzzled. "What makes you think I'd have a problem with it?"

"Well." He glanced over his shoulder to make sure the kids were still in the truck and the windows were rolled up. He didn't want to have to answer their questions if they overheard this. "You remember how weird things got after we had that threesome with that guy?"

Michelle slowly nodded. "Yeah ..."

"Well, you said some stuff that made me wonder ..."

"Oh." She covered her mouth with her hand. "Oh, no, Adrian ... I ... Shit. Okay. Let me explain. I was feeling pretty crappy about myself at that point. I'd had two babies in just under three years. I was stressed and frazzled like any parent. You were gone all the time at the bakery. I felt terrible about my body, and here was this gorgeous guy who you were so into, and ... I got insecure. I started worrying you'd leave me for him and just walk out of all of our lives and leave me with two kids and ..." She wiped at her watering eyes. "I know you'd never do that to me, much less the kids. All of that was irrational, but I probably said some things I shouldn't have because of my insecurities."

"Oh, shit, Michelle, I had no idea." He reached out automatically to hug her, and she squeezed him tight for a second before she stepped back. "I never wanted you to feel like that. Yeah, I enjoyed being with that guy, but it wasn't because he was somehow better than you. Or more attractive."

"Well, in hindsight, I know that. And I should have talked to you about how I was feeling at the time," she admitted. "But communication was not our strong suit at that point."

"No, it wasn't," he agreed. "I am sorry, though."

"And I'm sorry you ever thought I had a problem with you being bi." She let out a little sigh. "God, I had no idea it came across that way."

"Maybe I leaped to conclusions."

She gave him a rueful little smile. "Story of our lives together, right? We assumed things without doing a good job of talking them through."

He nodded. "I'm glad we're doing better now."

"I am too." She wrapped her sweater around her a little tighter. "We can talk more another time, if you'd like, but I'm freezing, and you look like you're about to fall over from exhaustion, so you should get out of here. Just know I have no problem with you dating a man. If you can work things out with this guy you reconnected with, or start dating someone else, I'll be happy for you. You deserve it."

"Thanks, Michelle." He hugged her again. "That means a lot."

"Of course, Adrian." She squeezed him tightly for a minute, and a feeling of peace settled over him. "I know things were rough when we first split, but you're a great dad to our kids, and I can honestly say there's no one I'd rather co-parent with."

He gave her a small smile and turned away, too choked up to answer. After years of fighting while they were married and a tense past year as they slowly figured these new interactions out, it felt good to walk away feeling better about their relationship.

He might have fucked things up with Jay past any hope of repair, but maybe having a solid parenting relationship with his ex-wife was enough for now.

———

Adrian pulled into the driveway of his home with a relieved sigh. While he'd had a good time in Philly with Seth and enjoyed the brief break from work and taking care of the kids, he had missed being home.

He put the truck in park. Although the house had a garage, it was tucked under the front of the house and built in the 1930s, so it was much too small for his vehicle. He got out, then helped the kids unload their bags and his own. They raced ahead to the front door, but he followed a little more slowly.

His place was just a few blocks from his parents' house and in the same school district as the one the kids were currently in. There had been nothing available for sale in the area in his price range, so he'd had to rent.

The current owners, an older couple, whom his parents had known for years, had bought it years ago and maintained it well as a rental property, but they were looking to move to Florida in the next few years and planned to sell it before then. He was hopeful that as the bakery grew, he might be able to buy it.

He'd been happy here since the divorce. The two-story brick house with the sharply peaked roof was small and cozy with three tiny bedrooms and one and a half baths. The kids loved the yard, and while the kitchen was a little cramped, there was space to expand in the yard if he decided to buy the house and stay there permanently.

Adrian tried to listen closely to Molly's excited chatter about her day as he unlocked the arched door and pushed it open. They all dropped their bags on the wood floor just inside the door, and Adrian breathed a sigh of relief at the familiar smell of home.

"So, did you do all your homework?" he asked. He stooped down to help Josh with his shoelace that had become knotted.

"Yep!" Molly said.

"Me too!" Josh piped up.

"Good." Adrian opened the closet door so they could hang up their coats and put away their shoes. "And you had dinner?"

"Mom made chicken and broccoli, and I ate it all!" Josh boasted.

Adrian chuckled. He'd never met a kid who loved broccoli as much as Josh. His little weirdo. "Awesome. I kinda wish I'd had some. I just had a burger, and it wasn't very good."

Adrian hadn't had the emotional wherewithal to find a healthy meal along the way, so he'd drowned his misery in greasy beef, onion rings, and a vat of caffeine in the form of Coke to keep him awake on the drive. Of course, now that it had worn off, he felt sluggish *and* unsatisfied. Gross.

He gently herded the kids forward, then put away his own things. "Okay, it's getting late. I need you to brush your teeth and get ready for bed, Josh. I'll be up to read to you as soon as you're done. Molly, make sure your backpack is packed and pick out your clothes for school. You can read until I come up to tuck you in."

Molly took off like a rocket, but Josh dawdled. "Go on, kiddo," Adrian urged. "Or you'll be tired in the morning."

"I missed you, Daddy."

Adrian swept him up in a hug. "Aww, I missed you too, kiddo."

———

A short while later, Josh was asleep in his bedroom with the glow-in-the-dark solar system on the ceiling. Adrian walked down the hall to peek his head into Molly's bedroom. "Ready for bed?"

"Yup." She waved the book she'd been reading at him. "Can I finish the chapter?"

"Sure." He still read to her sometimes, but more and more, she wanted to do it on her own. She was growing up so fast. He spotted her backpack on the floor, and the clothes she'd picked out for the next day on her dresser, so he had no problem giving her a few more minutes to read. He walked over to the window that overlooked the back yard and stared out into the dark night while she finished.

If Adrian closed his eyes, he could picture Jay slotting into their lives. On a night like this, he might be downstairs watching basketball while Adrian tucked the kids in. Adrian could imagine walking into the living room and seeing Jay sprawled on the couch, smiling at him. Adrian would settle in on the couch beside Jay for a quiet evening in. But at some point, one of them would say something that ignited a fire in the other, and they'd make out on the couch before they went upstairs to their bedroom. They'd have to be quiet when they made love so as not to wake the kids, but they'd certainly managed to be stealthy this past week ...

The image dissolved like smoke as he remembered Jay didn't want that.

Jay didn't trust him.

Maybe Adrian should have seen it coming, but he hadn't, and the news had completely blindsided him. He felt a flicker of anger as he wondered if Jay had deliberately had sex with him as payback. He couldn't get past that thought. He didn't want to believe it, and Jay's wide-eyed surprised when he accused him had seemed genuine, but Adrian found it difficult to trust.

Trust. There was that fucking word again.

Was it his own guilt talking like Jay had suggested? Adrian had fucked Jay over in the past, so now he assumed that Jay had done the same? Did believing Jay was no better than him soothe his own guilt? Maybe. Probably. Adrian didn't know anymore. All he knew was that it felt like there was a very large hole in his life that might never go away.

"Daddy?" Molly's voice broke him from his thoughts. "Are you okay?"

"Sorry, kiddo." He turned to face the bed and managed a weak smile. "Yeah, I'm okay. I was just thinking about a friend I saw in Philadelphia."

"Uncle Seth?"

He laughed and took a seat on the end of the bed. "No, not Uncle Seth or Uncle Erik. Someone I met last year." Adrian's throat went tight, and he struggled to keep the waver out of his voice. "Do you remember when I spent the weekend in New York at the baking conference?"

"Yep."

"Well, I met someone there. A pastry chef named Jay." Adrian didn't know why he was telling his daughter all of this. It wasn't like it mattered. Like she'd ever meet Jay. A thought occurred to

Adrian. Shit that wasn't true. Molly would definitely meet Jay this summer at Seth and Erik's wedding. And worst of all, Jay and Adrian would have to work together on the cake. He'd nearly forgotten. Which meant that sometime in the near future, Adrian would have to contact Jay to discuss their plans for the cake. *Fuuuck.*

Molly was still staring expectantly, so he cleared his throat. "Jay is a friend of your Uncle Seth. They used to be roommates. You'll get to meet Jay at the wedding this summer."

"Do I get to be in the wedding?" Molly asked, sitting up. "Like a flower girl or something?"

"Hmm, I don't know. I'll have to ask Seth about that. I do know I'm going to be his best man, and I'm making him a cake."

"Is it going to be a yummy cake?

Adrian placed his hands on his hips and faked a look of outrage. "Have I ever made a cake that wasn't yummy?"

"Yes," Molly said decisively. "It was gross that time you burned my birthday cake."

Adrian groaned. "I'd forgotten about that." It had been right after he had told Michelle he wanted the divorce, and he'd been so distracted he'd forgotten to set a timer. It hadn't been totally burned, but there was charring on the edges that he tried to cut off. It hadn't been very successful, and Molly had taken one bite and made a face. She'd had a meltdown over it, and Adrian had nearly done the same. He felt like he was letting down his whole family, and the spoiled birthday cake had been the proverbial icing on top of the cake. It had *not* been a good time in his life.

"It's okay. You made me another one," Molly said, her tone philosophical.

Adrian leaned down and hugged her. "I did. And I promise I won't burn Uncle Seth's wedding cake."

"Yay!"

Adrian laughed. "Okay, time for bed, kiddo. You've got school tomorrow."

Molly gave him a long-suffering sigh but settled back against the pillows. Adrian smoothed her brown curls out of the way, then kissed her forehead. "Sleep tight."

"Night, Daddy."

"G'night."

Adrian pulled the door closed behind him, then walked downstairs to make lunches and lock up before bed. Exhaustion was beginning to hit him already, and he was sure he'd fall asleep as soon as his head hit the pillow.

But despite his exhaustion, forty-five minutes later, Adrian was still staring up at the ceiling. He'd gone through his evening routine and climbed into bed, but now, he lay there wondering why he couldn't sleep. He glanced over at the pillow beside him. Damn it. He knew why. He missed Jay. Just a couple nights sleeping beside Jay and he was already used to it.

But the more he thought about it, the more Jay's earlier words had begun to make sense. How could Adrian have expected Jay to just drop everything to be with him? What had Adrian done to prove that he deserved that? A couple days of great sex weren't enough when Adrian had done nothing but betray Jay's trust. If their positions were reversed, would Adrian trust anyone who treated him the way Adrian had treated Jay? Of course not.

Jesus, he was getting stupider by the day.

The best he could hope for was that in a month or two, after things were a little less raw, he could contact Jay about baking the wedding cake for Seth and Erik. Not with any hidden agenda or a plan to try to win him back. It hurt, but he could admit he didn't deserve another chance. No, he had to try to be friends with Jay. Because it was the best thing for Jay.

It was too late for Adrian to fix his past mistakes, but he could be a goddamn grownup and stop doing things that hurt Jay.

Adrian flipped onto his side, missing Jay's warmth. His bed was cozy and familiar, but it wasn't the same as sharing it with Jay. In the dark, Adrian closed his eyes, knowing he'd made the right decision to focus on a friendship with Jay but feeling the sting of tears at the loss of anything more. It was going to be a long time before Adrian stopped feeling shitty about the way things had gone down.

And he had no one to blame but himself.

ELEVEN

"Hey, boss," Henry said.

Adrian looked up from his clipboard at his assistant manager. He was tall and lanky, with a short gray-flecked beard that he kept neatly trimmed. He always looked a little hangdog and miserable, but he was one of the steadiest, most reliable employees Adrian had ever had. He was the only reason Adrian had been able to take time off to help Seth move.

"You ready for the big day tomorrow? Henry asked.

"Ugh, I hope so. Everything's set to go for the big launch of the pistachio-rose cupcakes, and it's just in time for Valentine's Day, so hopefully, they sell well."

"They're the bomb," Henry said. "Seriously, next-level stuff."

Adrian nodded. He agreed but the cupcakes brought up a strange mix of feelings in him. It had been a week since he'd gotten back from Philly, and the sting of missing Jay hadn't faded at all. He still fell asleep thinking about Jay and woke up missing him.

And planning for tomorrow's romantic holiday hadn't helped. They'd decorated the front of the bakery today. Well, Sasha, a college student who worked the counter part-time, had. She'd been enthusiastic about it, and Adrian had been happy to hand it over. The last thing he wanted to think about was a day to celebrate love. He'd never been that crazy about Valentine's Day to begin with. Partly because he'd always worked long hours and Michelle had been annoyed that he never had the energy to celebrate after he got home. Most years, it just felt like a cheap, commercial holiday designed to make people overspend on flowers, chocolates, and engagement rings.

But since it was a big day for the bakery, and he was hoping this year would bring his best sales ever, he'd let Sasha go all out. Adrian had never gotten around to taking down the white lights he'd draped around the front windows at Christmas. And despite Adrian's grumpiness about the holiday, even he could admit the lights looked nice with the garlands of hearts Sasha had added. The window display had touches of red and pink, and she'd added hearts and flowers to the big chalkboard menu on the wall.

Heart-shaped cakes with white, pink, and red frosting were lined up in the coolers, along with shortbread cookies that resembled conversation hearts with romantic messages piped onto them. Adrian had raspberry-topped cheesecakes and chocolate cherry sheet cakes ready for the next day. And the pistachio-rose cupcakes were the showstopper.

In short, he had everything ready for a day of love, except the person to celebrate it with.

No, that wasn't true—he had the kids, and they'd be over-the-moon excited by the treats he planned to bring home for them tomorrow. But no matter how loved he was by his kids or his family, it was clear there was something missing. And that something was Jay. Adrian sighed.

Adrian ticked off the second to last thing on his To Do list, then looked at what he had left. Check Instagram and reply to messages. He'd taken a bunch of photos in the past week and put them up with the list of hashtags Seth had sent him.

Ugh. He still hated the social media thing, but Seth had been right. He was already starting to see results. He'd even gotten that stupid little light, which somehow did make all of the pictures he took look bright and perfectly lit. Admitting his brother was right wasn't easy, but he'd sent Seth a grudging thank you the other day.

Now, when he logged in, he saw 333 new likes.

Adrian blinked. Well, that was new. Usually, it was just a few here and there. Yesterday he'd had two dozen when he checked at the end of the day. He scrolled through them, liking and replying to a few comments.

He paused when he saw a notification. *@The Wanderer tagged you in a post.* That was Seth's username. Adrian clicked on it and stared down at the photo of his pistachio-rose cupcakes that Seth had finally gotten around to posting. Wow. Adrian's cupcakes had never looked so good. The light hit them just right, highlighting every swirl in the frosting and made his mouth water. He could almost taste the silky-sweet frosting on the tip of his tongue ... and then his mind replaced it with the taste of Jay's mouth, the hint of frosting adding a delicious richness to the kiss. If he closed his eyes, he could feel Jay's hands on his hips and his thigh slotting between Adrian's. He could smell the warm, masculine scent he wore and feel the slippery silk of Jay's hair between his fingers ...

"Did you doze off there, boss?" Henry sounded amused.

Adrian cleared his throat. "Uh, no." He stuffed his phone in his pocket. He'd look more closely at the cupcake post later. When he was alone. Because it wasn't creepy and weird at all to masturbate to a photo of cupcakes. He stifled a groan. He was getting more and more pathetic by the day. Adrian cleared his throat again. "Looks like we're all set for tomorrow if you want to head out, Henry."

"Sounds good. See you tomorrow."

"Get some sleep," Adrian said. "It's going to be a long one."

"Holidays always are!" Henry said. A rare smile crossed his face. "But it's worth it."

"It is," Adrian agreed. On holidays, he easily made three to four times the usual number of daily sales. He'd already ordered a lunch to be catered in for his employees as a thank you. It was just a variety of sandwiches and wraps, a few sides, and drinks from a local deli, but it always boosted morale and kept everybody going. When they were all busting their butts for him, it was the least he could do.

"Night, Adrian!" Henry called as he walked through the back.

"Night!" he replied. He reached into the pastry case, then flicked out the light. He turned off the string lights by the window as well and checked to be sure the door was locked. Henry had put up the closed sign an hour ago. Adrian made his usual rounds to be sure everything was ready for the next day, locked the back door, then stepped outside into the crisp night air. They hadn't had any snow, but it had been chilly, and he burrowed his hands in his ever-present King of Tarts hoodie as he walked to his truck. He didn't have the kids for a few days. Michelle had them tonight, and Adrian's mom would pick them up at school tomorrow.

Adrian always felt bad he couldn't make it to the holiday parties at school. It bummed the kids out—and him too—but it helped to know their mom and grandma would be there. Sometimes, Adrian's dad or his nearby siblings, Mitchell and Sarah, often filled in too. Plus Michelle's parents. Honestly, he was lucky to have so many people in his life who looked out for him and his kids.

Adrian's house felt lonely when he stepped inside, though, and he ate leftovers in front of the TV as he watched basketball and tried not to think of Jay. Which reminded him, he hadn't responded to his brother's Instagram post.

He set his empty plate aside, then brought up the app. His lips curved in a smile as he read the caption on it.

Have you ever seen prettier cupcakes? I've been to nearly every continent in the world, but I don't think I ever have. And the good news is, they taste even better than they look!

So if you're ever near Pittsburgh, Pennsylvania be sure to check out the King of Tarts bakery. My little brother makes some seriously kick-ass cupcakes, and you won't regret making the trip!

There was a massive string of hashtags following that, and Adrian's eyes bugged out as he saw the number of likes and comments on the post. Holy shit. That was insane.

After some serious thought, Adrian finally managed a reply to Seth's post that didn't sound completely stupid and awkward, but as he scrolled through the other comments, one from someone with the username @JPastry caught his eye. Adrian quickly scanned the comment. *I can confirm. These are some of the most beautiful and delicious-tasting cupcakes I've ever had the privilege to try.*

Adrian's breath caught and his chest felt very full as he clicked on the profile to confirm it was Jay's. His heart beat fast at the sight of Jay's face in his icon photo. It meant a lot that Jay would praise Adrian's work and try to help promote him after the way things had ended. It didn't change anything, but Adrian held the knowledge close to his heart as he went to bed that night.

Friends. They could be friends. It didn't feel like enough, but it would have to be. He had to do what was best for Jay.

———

From the moment Adrian arrived at the bakery in the morning, he was in work-mode, and all thoughts of social media and Jay were pushed aside. Adrian had bread, doughnuts, and other treats to bake and decorate like always, and alongside two of his other bakers, he worked steadily to tick every item off the list in the hours before the bakery opened.

As Adrian slid another sheet pan of chocolate chip cookies into the oven, Henry appeared. Which meant they were opening in about twenty minutes. Henry always arrived an hour or two after Adrian because he closed up for the day while Adrian finished paperwork or went home to the kids.

"Uh, boss?"

"Yeah?" Adrian wiped sweat off his forehead with the back of his arm.

"There's a lineup this morning."

"What?"

"Like, thirty-some people are waiting outside." Adrian blinked. They occasionally had a few waiting outside when they opened. Usually, people planning to grab a few treats to take home after work or to their lucky co-workers. But thirty? He'd never had that many, even right before Christmas.

"For us?"

"Yep. They're all lined up, starting at our door."

"Holy shit. Well, okay. Looks like it's going to be a busy one today. You need any help out front, you let me know, okay?"

It was chaos the moment they opened.

The morning was a blur as everyone scrambled to keep up with the demand as person after person came in to order the pistachio-rose cupcakes. Adrian let his other bakers deal with everything else as he focused on the special flavor. He'd never anticipated going through this many in a single day, and he felt woefully unprepared. Thankfully, other employees had arrived to work the front of the bakery and handle the crowds.

It wasn't until lunchtime that Adrian had a chance to consider why they were so busy.

He munched on a turkey pesto wrap as he checked his phone for the first time that day. He took a peek at Instagram and nearly dropped his food when he spotted the number of notifications. *Holy fucking shit.* The pieces finally clicked into place. Seth. Seth was responsible for this insanity.

Adrian brought up his brother's number and hit send.

"Oh, my God, Seth, I am going to murder you," Adrian said as soon as he picked up. "Why did you have to pick yesterday of all days to do this?"

"Why? What's going on?" Seth sounded alarmed. "And what did I do?"

"The bakery is *swamped*. I have never seen it this busy. My employees and I have barely had time to breathe."

"How is that my fault?"

"Your cupcake post went fucking viral. Business is insane."

"Oh. Uh, you're welcome?" Seth sounded a little annoyed.

Adrian took a deep breath, reminding himself he shouldn't yell at his brother for doing something nice for him. "Don't get me wrong. I'm grateful. I'll probably be more grateful once I tally all the sales, but holy shit, I don't know if I can keep up! They are lined up around the block and have been all morning. We have nowhere near enough cupcakes made."

"Take a deep breath," Seth said.

"I can't! I have four hundred thousand cupcakes to bake!"

"So bake them! Yelling at me isn't going to get them done. I'd offer to help but ..."

"Yeah, you're a little far, and you're a menace to baked goods. I get it. Fine. Thank you for your post. I hate you a little bit, but I appreciate it. Or I will eventually."

"Any time."

"Ugh, warn a dude ahead of time, though."

"Where's the fun in that? Now go bake some damn cupcakes."

"Fuck you." Adrian hung up, knowing his brother was probably laughing at him.

———

Sasha poked her head in the back about an hour after lunch. "There's someone here to see you, Adrian."

"Seriously?" Adrian wiped at the sweat on his forehead with his arm for the umpteenth time that day.

"Yeah, he said it was important."

"Ugh. Okay. Uhh, tell him once I get these cupcakes in I'll be out."

Adrian lost himself in the familiar rhythm of measure, dump, stir. The industrial mixer whirred, and Adrian was too focused on not forgetting an ingredient to worry about who was there to see him.

But when he shut the machine off and twisted the bowl loose from the base, he frowned. Who on earth could it be? Sasha knew his whole family. They popped in all the time. And they rarely used the front door. They almost always came in through the back entrance, so he couldn't imagine they'd suddenly come through the front, especially when it was so busy. And Sasha would have mentioned them by name, anyway.

Maybe it was one of the neighboring shops complaining about the crowds? But that was odd too. They should be good with the increased foot traffic. Surely, some of the people had stopped into those shops too. And the flower shop three storefronts down was always packed on Valentine's Day anyway.

Adrian realized he'd been moving on autopilot, plopping cupcake liners into the tins and filling them with a large scoop. Good thing he could do this part without much concentration.

Maybe the owner of the flower shop was irritated by the extra vehicles parked in the lot behind the building. It wasn't unusual for their customers to spill over into Adrian's spaces, and he never complained about that. Turnabout really was fair play.

He scraped the last of the batter into the scoop, then plopped it into the final hole in the tin. Well, he'd find out soon enough. No point in worrying about it until he did.

A timer beeped just as he set the dirty scoop, bowl, and mixer attachment next to the sink. Time to get the previous batches out. It felt like a never-ending assembly line today.

He silenced the beeping, carefully pulled the hot trays from the oven, and slid them into an upright rack to cool. He set a timer for that, put the new batter-filled trays into the oven, set another timer, and then took a moment to stretch. Jesus, his shoulders felt like they were filled with knots that would never loosen. And his day wasn't over yet.

What was he doing? Oh, right, he needed to make the frosting. He pulled out egg whites, sugar, and butter and squinted at the supplies he had left. Shit, he'd never been this low on so many things at once before.

He'd just set out the last of the rosewater and cardamom when he heard Henry's raised voice. "You can't just go in there!"

"It's fine. Adrian knows me. And I'm a pastry chef." Adrian lifted his head, his eyes wide. He knew that voice. He definitely fucking knew that voice. But what the hell was Jay doing in Pittsburgh?

Adrian turned around to see Jay standing in the doorway of the kitchen, wearing a smile on his face and a holiday-appropriate red button-down shirt. Adrian had to blink a few times to be sure he hadn't hallucinated him like some sort of frosting-induced vision.

"Jay?" Adrian stared blankly at him. "What ... what are you *doing* here?"

"No time for that. What do you need help with?"

"What?"

"You're swamped. I have the skills to help. What do you need me to do?" His tone was crisp and no-nonsense, and it broke through the fog in Adrian's head.

"Uh, well, those cupcakes need to be iced as soon as they're fully cool." He pointed at the batch on the rack.

"Is the icing made? What kind of tip do you want me to use?"

"The rosewater Swiss meringue buttercream is right there." Adrian pointed to the bowl the previous batch was in. "Pastry bags and tips are there. Take your pick of styles. At this point, I'm less concerned about the specific style than getting the damn things done."

"Gonna grab an apron too, if that's okay." Jay gestured to his clothing. "I didn't exactly plan on working today."

"Uh, sure. Go for it."

Adrian watched for a second as Jay put on an apron, then scrubbed his hands at the sink. "I thought you had a lot to do," Jay threw over his shoulder.

"I do. I'm just trying to figure out what the hell you're doing here. I'm half-afraid if I blink you'll vanish."

"I'm here. And I'll explain it all in detail later. The short version is that I came to talk."

"So, you didn't show up to save my ass?"

"I didn't know your ass needed saving." Jay scooped a large dollop of the buttercream into a piping bag, then closed it with a practiced twist. "Now bake!"

"Yes, Chef!" With a shake of his head, Adrian got back to work, mixing the cupcakes. By the time he slid the batch in the oven and set the timer, there was a row of beautifully frosted cupcakes in front of Jay. He worked quickly and deftly. Adrian just watched him for a moment, totally overwhelmed but impressed.

"You're kind of a lifesaver, you know that?"

"I know." Jay didn't look up from the cupcake in his hand. "And you can express your undying gratitude to me later. But first, tell me why your bakery is exploding with people. I nearly got into a fistfight with someone who thought I was jumping the line. Your customers are fucking cutthroat."

"Uhh, that would be Seth," Adrian said with a sigh. "I love my brother but I could totally strangle him right now."

"What did he do?"

"Posted about the cupcakes on his Instagram yesterday. Some 'influencer' saw it and went apeshit over it. She came and got her own cupcake and posted about it this morning, and the whole thing blew up. The bakery has been slammed all day, and it doesn't show any sign of slowing down."

"Yeah, I saw Seth's post. The pictures do look amazing. Couldn't help but notice what flavor you're selling boatloads of today too," Jay said. He sounded so relaxed and easy, and Adrian's head was still spinning at the thought that he was there. And helping. And he didn't seem angry. Had Adrian stumbled into some alternate dimension or something?

"Uh, yeah. I owe you big time for your flavor suggestion. I have never even remotely come close to selling this many of *anything* in one day."

"Well, the sales numbers are all thanks to Seth, but I'm glad I could help you create a flavor that people are into." Jay gave him a little wink before his expression grew serious. "Should we make some more batches?"

"I don't know if we *can*. I'm nearly out of at least three different ingredients." Adrian held up the bottle of rosewater and sloshed around the remaining teaspoon.

"Better see if your supplier can get you some tomorrow."

"We're closed tomorrow. Thank God. But you're right. I should still call, in case people show up the day after looking for them. Who knows, though? Maybe it'll be a flash in the pan, and people will get bored with it in twenty-four hours."

"I don't know." Jay scraped the spoon across the side of the bowl to pick up the remnants, then licked the frosting off it. "It's pretty amazing stuff."

"It is, isn't it?" Adrian smiled at him.

Once the final batch of pistachio cupcakes was cool, they fell into a rhythm with Jay frosting and Adrian sprinkling them with the chopped pistachios, then topping them with a candied rose petal.

"What time do you close?" Jay asked after Adrian had carried the final tray out to the front of the bakery.

Adrian glanced at the clock on the wall. "Two hours from now. And I can't believe how packed it still is out there."

"Better hope you have enough cupcakes to last until then." Jay frowned. "What about doing another flavor you *do* have the ingredients for? Something equally delicious might appease people when you tell them you're out of your signature flavor."

"I can't just create something brand new on the fly!" Adrian protested, a sense of panic overwhelming him for a moment. "It takes me weeks, sometimes more, to develop new recipes."

"Hey. Take a deep breath," Jay said firmly, and Adrian dutifully sucked some air into his lungs. "Okay, now tell me what cupcake and frosting flavors you already make. Maybe we can make a minor tweak or combine them in new and different ways without having to worry about creating something completely brand new."

After Adrian rattled off the list of flavors, Jay hummed thoughtfully. "Okay. Well, I might combine the lemon cupcakes with the dark chocolate icing, but that doesn't feel quite right for Valentine's Day. Let me think. What about ... dark chocolate cupcakes stuffed with cream cheese filling and a cherry frosting? Sort of a chocolate cherry cheesecake flavor. It's not terribly unusual, but it might do the trick. And it certainly suits the holiday."

"I like that," Adrian said slowly, thinking about what ingredients he had available. "What if we flipped it, though? I think I have some leftover cherry filling I made this morning for the mini cheesecakes we're selling. And then we could just do the chocolate cupcakes and a quick cream cheese frosting but add a dash of amaretto for interest. Some chocolate shavings and a cherry on top should make it fancy enough for Instagram."

"I like it." Jay grinned at him. "Come on, let's get to work."

They worked together quickly and when the timer on the final batch of chocolate cupcakes beeped, Adrian let out a relieved sigh. "Thank God. Let's get these stupid things frosted and get them out front."

"After today, I don't think I'll be able to stand looking at another cupcake. Ever," Jay muttered.

"I'm in total agreement. And I have to sell the damn things."

When the cupcakes were done and in Sasha's hands at the front of the bakery, Adrian returned to the kitchen, feeling completely wrung out.

Jay had collapsed onto a stool and was slumped on it like he'd never get up again. "And I thought working in a restaurant kitchen was bad. Jesus, what kind of masochist are you?"

Adrian chuckled as he fell heavily into the chair next to him. "It's not always this bad."

"It might be if you keep this up."

"I think I'm going to need to hire some additional people if I do," Adrian said wearily. He let his head loll to the side so he could look at Jay. "You still looking for a job?"

Yes." Jay grinned. "I'm not quite that desperate though, thanks."

Which reminded Adrian, he still had no idea what Jay was doing here. "So why are you here in Pittsburgh anyway?"

"I'm ..." Jay leaned forward and braced his forearms on his thighs. "Shit, this wasn't how I'd planned to tell you, Adrian."

"Tell me what?"

"Tell you I'm sorry about the way I left things between us in Philly."

"Oh." Adrian blinked at him. "You could have just called or texted or something. Unless you deleted my number?"

"No, I still have it. I figured what I had to say needed to be said face-to-face, though."

"Okay." Adrian wet his lips. "So, here I am. Talk to me."

"When you left Philly, I really thought I was doing the right thing. It all made sense in my head to just end things then and go our separate ways."

"I fucking hated it," Adrian admitted. "But after I got home and had some time to let the sting of it all fade, I understood where you were coming from."

"The funny thing is I started to have doubts. And your brother and I talked for a little while."

"He's a good listener," Adrian said.

"It was less listening and more him telling me I'm an idiot." Jay's tone was dry.

"He's even better at that."

Jay shot him a small smile. "He is. Because he wasn't wrong. I was an idiot for letting you go and maybe too hasty when I made my decision."

"You were right that I'm tied to living in Pittsburgh, though," Adrian said. "I mean, I can't leave my kids or the bakery so ..." He lifted his shoulders in a helpless shrug. "A long-distance relationship would be really fucking hard on both of us, especially because you'd be the one traveling most of the time. Even if you're in Philly rather than New York, that's not a quick drive. It's five hours. And by the time you figure in dealing with security at an airport ... flying isn't much faster. That's a lot to put on you. And it's not like you have an easy job, and you couldn't just take off time at a new place and—"

"Whoa, Adrian, slow down. I don't need you to talk me out of a long-distance relationship. You already did that once."

Adrian pressed his lips tightly together. Was that what he'd been doing? God, he was an idiot too. Although that was hardly news. "Sorry," he muttered.

"In the end, it wasn't really about all of the obstacles we'd have to overcome. It was about *me*. I was just scared, I guess. It felt so natural to be with you again, but I was fucking terrified you were going to pull the plug on things again once we were apart, and I just …" Jay sighed. "I guess I figured you couldn't hurt me if I hurt you first."

"Oh, Jay." Adrian felt stricken.

"So, you were partially right. It was sort of payback. I wasn't trying to do it but …"

"It's not like anyone can blame you for being a little gun-shy, least of all me."

"I know. But it's pretty stupid to ruin something good just because I'm scared."

"Okay," Adrian said slowly as he tried to understand what Jay was getting at. "But what does that mean for us exactly?"

"Well, I was thinking …" Jay cleared his throat. "I was wondering if you were still willing to hook me up with that guy you know here in Pittsburgh."

"Here in Pittsburgh …" Adrian frowned, then realization dawned, and he sat up straight. "Wait, you mean you're thinking of moving here?"

"If the offer still stands?" Jay gave him a tentative smile. "It was a good suggestion. I was just too overwhelmed to consider it when you brought it up last week."

"It was pretty out of the blue," Adrian agreed. "I can understand why you didn't want to just agree to uproot your entire life for some guy."

"But you're not some guy." Jay reached out and took his hand. "You're a pretty great guy. One I really care about. Not perfect but neither am I. We've both got our baggage I guess, but I'd like to fix things between us if I can. What do you say?"

"I ... Yeah, of course, I want that, Jay. But I want you to know that no matter what happens between us, I'll help you find a job, okay?"

"That's probably more than I deserve after how hot and cold I was last week."

"Yeah, well, I fucked up even worse last year so ..." Adrian shook his head. "Look, I'm not trying to keep score here. I care about you, Jay. We have some real potential together. If we're both on the same page about giving it a try, I want to go for it," he said firmly.

"I do too." Jay gave him a small smile.

Adrian smiled back, but it dipped when he remembered something. "What about trusting me? Because I don't blame you for being worried about that. I haven't been very trustworthy."

"Honestly, I think maybe I've been looking at this all wrong. No, I don't fully trust you. *Yet.* But trust isn't something that happens overnight. It's something that takes time. After I thought about it, I realized it wouldn't happen at all unless I make a leap of faith. I've been looking for a fresh start. There's no reason I can't do that in Pittsburgh, assuming I can find a job here. Even if things don't work out between us, I'd still have my career. I can still make friends and establish a life here either way."

"Hey, before you start breaking us up, let's try dating first," Adrian said, trying to inject a little humor in the conversation.

The corner of Jay's mouth curled up. "I like the sound of that."

"Me too." Adrian stood and walked over to Jay, tugging him to his feet. He wrapped his arms around Jay's waist and pulled him close. Adrian studied his face, looking into his dark brown eyes, then tracing his stubbled jaw with his gaze.

Jay gave him a sweet smile. "You look like you're trying to memorize me."

"Maybe I am," Adrian admitted. "I can barely believe this is happening right now. I really thought I'd lost you for good."

"I'm not going anywhere." Jay smoothed a hand across the back of Adrian's head before sliding it down so his palm rested against the back of his neck. It sent a pleasant shiver through Adrian's body. "In fact, now that I've seen how crazy busy you are here at the bakery, I think maybe I should help you out here for a short while. Just until I find something more permanent and you hire someone new."

"You don't want to work for me full-time?" Adrian teased. He didn't mean it, though. Although they both enjoyed baking desserts, their interests and talents were different. Besides, it wasn't fair to expect him to step aside and take orders from Adrian when he was used to running the show in his own kitchen. Or at least, the baking side of things. Deferring to Adrian was too likely to put a strain on their relationship, and Adrian very much wanted to give it the best possible shot to work.

"I don't want a full-time job frosting cupcakes." There was humor in Jay's voice too. "But I'm happy to help you out for a little bit. Just until things settle down."

"I'd appreciate that." Adrian leaned in a little closer. "And I don't mind the thought of working side by side with you."

"Mmm, good." Jay brushed their lips together. "Because I can think of all sorts of things I'd like to work on very, very closely together with you."

"I like the sound of that even more." Adrian pressed his lips to Jay's, but before he could deepen the kiss, the sound of his employee's voice made him start.

"Hey, boss, it looks like we're finally—Oh! Shit. Sorry, didn't mean to interrupt."

Damn it. Adrian tried to remember it was a bad idea to kill his best employee. He lifted his head and stepped back from Jay but not too far. He didn't let go of his waist because he definitely wanted to keep touching Jay. And his staff already knew he was bi. "What were you saying, Henry?"

Henry shuffled awkwardly. "Oh, uh, we finally locked up behind the last customer."

"Oh, thank God." Adrian looked skyward. "I'm sure you're at least as exhausted as I am, if not more so."

"It's been a long day," Henry agreed. "But, hey, that was—without question—a record sales day. By a huge margin. The drawers are stuffed full of cash, and the pile of credit card slips is unreal. I haven't had a chance to tally it but ..."

"It's going to be great," Adrian said with a grin. "And let me tell you, everyone who worked today is getting a bonus as a thank you for all their hard work."

"Awesome. I won't argue with that." Henry grinned back. It was the happiest Adrian had ever seen him.

Adrian sighed as reality hit. "But now we need to clean up, and I need to call the supplier about what we need to re-stock. Thank God, we're closed tomorrow, but the day after is likely to be nuts."

"I've got it. Why don't you get out of here, boss?" Henry's gaze flicked between him and Jay. "It looks like you have Valentine's Day plans after all."

"Are you sure you don't mind?"

"Nope. I took care of all of it while you were in Philly, and you seemed happy with the job I did."

"I was," Adrian agreed. "I know you can handle it. I just don't want to take advantage of you."

"It's all good," Henry said. "My girlfriend works late tonight, so we planned to celebrate tomorrow anyway."

"If you're sure …"

"Absolutely. As soon as I have all of the info for the supplier, you should head out."

"I can do that," Adrian said, feeling relieved. "Thanks."

TWELVE

Twenty minutes later, Adrian led Jay out through the back of the bakery to where his truck was parked. He paused beside it, considering what they should do next. "Well, I don't know about you, but I'm hungry."

"Starved."

"What are you in the mood for?"

"Anything that isn't covered in frosting."

Adrian chuckled. "Sounds good to me too. I'd offer to make you something, but I'm wrecked. Take you out to dinner instead?" he offered.

"I'd like that, but it's Valentine's Day. It's going to be a nightmare to get in anywhere."

Adrian groaned. "Damn it, you're right."

"How do you feel about frozen pizza?" Jay asked, wrapping his arms around Adrian to pull him close.

Adrian let out a little sigh of contentment. "If it's with you, it sounds perfect to me." Adrian slid a hand through Jay's hair and teased his tongue at the seam of Jay's lips. Jay groaned and let him in, kissing Adrian back with a ferocity that made his head spin. Food? Who needed food when he could have Jay?

A small giggle pierced through the fog he was in. "I think Daddy has a boyfriend."

Adrian stilled. *Welp, that's one way to officially introduce my kids to Jay.* Adrian lifted his head and met Jay's horrified expression. He gave him a reassuring smile, then stepped away. He kept his hand on Jay's back, though.

"Well, I didn't expect to see any of you here," Adrian said with another smile, this one wider as he looked at his kids and his mom. "What are you all doing here?"

"We thought you'd probably be hungry and would have to work late so we brought you dinner," his mother said. Her gaze flicked over to Jay. "We didn't realize you had a date tonight, though."

"It was a little unexpected," Adrian said. "Jay came in from out of town."

"Would you like to introduce us?" she prompted.

Molly giggled again.

"Jay, this is my mom, Miranda Cobb, my daughter Molly, and my son Josh. Mom, Molly, Josh, this is Ajay Sunagar."

"Hi, Jay! Are you Daddy's boyfriend?" Molly asked.

"I—" Jay cleared his throat. "I think so?" He glanced over at Adrian, as if for confirmation.

"He is," Adrian said firmly. "Or, at least, I'd like him to be. We're going to start dating and see how it goes." He squeezed Jay's hand in reassurance. "It's all kinda new."

"Where did you meet?" Mrs. Cobb asked.

"At the baking expo in New York last year," Adrian said.

"Oh, you've been seeing each other that long?" She shot Adrian a pointed look. "Why on earth didn't you tell us?"

"Oh, no." Adrian floundered, unsure how to explain the situation.

"We met then and hit it off," Jay explained smoothly. "But the timing wasn't right because of the distance. We ran into each other again recently. Seth was my roommate in New York until he moved in with Erik. Adrian and I reconnected then. Adrian told me about some job opportunities here in Pittsburgh that I came to explore, and ... well, we're going to see how it goes."

"And just in time for Valentine's Day! How lovely." Miranda beamed at them both.

"It was quite a romantic surprise," Adrian agreed. "Especially because Jay is a pastry chef, and he pitched in today to help with the craziness."

"Oh, yes, I'm not surprised you were swamped. I heard about your cupcakes on the local news earlier, sweetie."

"The bakery was on the news?" Adrian felt a little dumbfounded.

Miranda laughed. "It was all over it. I think you'd better brace yourself for some more busy days. Your brother seems to have started something."

"Oh, shit," Adrian muttered. "Uh, Jay, I am *definitely* going to need your help until I can get some new people in here."

"Yeah, of course. I already told you I would."

"Would you like me to keep the kids tonight?" Miranda asked. "So you and Jay can have a little time to enjoy your evening and reconnect?"

"Uh, that would be nice." Adrian looked at Molly and Josh. "Are you guys okay with staying over at Grandma's?"

"Duh," Molly said. "She lets us have hot cocoa and as much popcorn as we want."

Adrian snorted. "Well, I see where I stand. Can I have a hug first, though?"

He knelt down and a minute later, and two small bodies thudded against him. He squeezed them tight. "Hey, can I talk to you guys seriously for a quick second? I know we'd discussed that at some point I might date someone other than your mom. If I'd known Jay was going to come visit and that you guys would be here, I would have told you he was coming. I didn't mean to surprise you with this."

"It's okay." Molly patted his cheek. "Mom's had a boyfriend for *ages*. You're just really behind."

"Thanks, kiddo." Adrian chuckled and squeezed her tighter. "You okay with it, Josh?"

He snuck a glance at Jay as if assessing him, then nodded.

"Good. Now I will see you tomorrow. Have a good night and be good for Grandma, okay?"

"Okay," they chorused.

Adrian gave them each one last squeeze and a kiss on the top of the head before he let go.

"Here's the food I made for you. A tray of manicotti, homemade breadsticks, and a salad."

"Oh, yum." Adrian's mouth watered as he took the canvas bag of food. "It's been forever since Dad's made manicotti."

"He thought you'd appreciate it after a day like today." She kissed Adrian's cheek, then turned to Jay. "It's nice to meet you. When things have settled down a little, I'd love to have you both over for dinner."

"That would be great," Jay said. "And it was very nice to meet you too."

Mrs. Cobb put her hands on Molly and Josh's backs and steered them toward her vehicle. "Come on, kids. Why don't we let your dad and Jay enjoy their date night now?"

"Okay. Goodnight!" Molly scampered off before she abruptly stopped and turned around.

"Wait! Would you like a candy heart?" Molly asked earnestly as she produced a bag from her coat pocket. She held it out to Jay. "I got so many today."

"I would love one," Jay said. He sounded just as earnest.

Molly beamed. "Let me pick a special one for you."

———

An hour or so later, Jay and Adrian sat on Adrian's couch, scraping their plates clean. The food had hit the spot. And if Adrian was too tired to move, well, that was okay. Jay was next to him and their sides were pressed together from their shoulders to their ankles. There was nowhere else Adrian wanted to be.

"So, your kids clearly know you're bi," Jay said.

"Yep." Adrian licked his fingers. *Mmm, garlic butter.* "They knew their Uncle Seth was gay, so from very early on, I explained that Daddy liked both boys and girls. It never phased them. I want my kids to know what's out there, you know? So they never have to question it or wonder if I'm okay with who they are."

"That makes sense." Jay stacked his plate on top of Adrian's on the coffee table. When he settled back, their shoulders brushed, and Adrian leaned in again with a contented sigh.

"And they seem cool with the idea of you dating again?"

"Yeah. That could have gone either way, honestly," Adrian admitted. "It was very possible they could have hated the idea, but they know when I'm happy. And there's no question I'm happier now than I was with Michelle. And she's happier now too. So they seem to be all right with the idea of us moving on with other people. I can't promise we won't run into any snags along the way, but ... that's life with kids, you know?" He turned to look at Jay, whose expression turned troubled.

"I guess." Jay smoothed his shirt down, and Adrian saw his fingers trembling. "Oh, Jesus, it's just hitting me all of a sudden."

"What's hitting you all of a sudden?" Adrian frowned.

"That you have kids. That I'll be dating a guy with kids. I mean, I have before, but they were in their teens, and this feels bigger somehow."

"Uhh, you aren't having second thoughts, are you?" Apprehension churned in Adrian's gut, and it wasn't a good feeling, especially after a plateful of food.

Jay sat up straight and looked over at him. "What? No. Of course not. It just occurred to me I know nothing about dating a guy with little kids. I don't have a clue what I'm doing."

Adrian rested his hand on Jay's thigh. "You don't have to have it all figured out. It's not like I'm going to throw you headlong into it," he explained patiently. "The kids will get to know you a little. We'll start with dinner, maybe a trip to the zoo after that ... And if things go the way I hope, slowly but surely, you'll become a bigger part of our day-to-day lives. It'll be gradual though. I promise I won't push you into the deep end."

Jay let out a heavy breath. "Yeah, okay. I can do that." Jay still sounded a little shaky, though, so Adrian leaned in and kissed him.

"You've got this. I know it. And we'll figure it out together, okay?"

"Okay."

Adrian stood and held out a hand to Jay. "Now, I don't know about you, but I'd like to go wash off the smell of frosting and garlic."

Jay took his hand and let Adrian pull him to his feet. "Hold that thought for a moment. You didn't happen to bring any of that leftover amaretto cream cheese frosting home, did you?"

Adrian chuckled. "In the chaos of everything that happened tonight, I'm afraid I forgot to grab it from the cooler."

"Damn. We never *did* get to lick frosting off each other, you know?"

Adrian turned to face him with a smile. "Well, there's always tomorrow."

Jay's face lit up. "There is."

"And hopefully, the one after that." Adrian squeezed Jay's hand.

"I'd like that." He squeezed back.

"Happy Valentine's Day, by the way," Adrian said as he leaned in for a kiss. "I think I officially have a new favorite holiday."

Chuckling, Jay cupped his cheek. "Happy Valentine's Day."

THIRTEEN

In the weeks after Valentine's Day, Jay found a small apartment about twenty minutes from Adrian's place. Together, they moved his belongings in. Adrian emailed his friend at Le Cordon Bleu about which restaurants in Pittsburgh were hiring. Two suggestions immediately appeared in his inbox, and Jay interviewed with both. Two excellent offers came in, and by the end of Jay's first month in Pittsburgh, he started a position at one of them.

Jay's help at King of Tarts for that first month was invaluable too because the bakery was doing a booming business.

There were a few minor bumps, but overall, the kids took to Jay quite quickly, which didn't surprise Adrian because Molly and Josh were both open and friendly, and Jay worked to find things he had in common with them.

But there was one thing that Adrian could never have predicted.

He arrived home from work to find Jay and Michelle chatting in the living room.

"Is everything okay, Michelle?" he asked as he came in. He'd spotted her minivan parked out front. She had a key to the house, and she occasionally came in if she brought the kids by before Adrian was home, but she rarely lingered.

She and Jay both glanced up at Adrian. "Oh, you're home, Adrian."

He gave her a puzzled smile. "Yep. I do live here …"

"I know that." Michelle laughed and glanced at her phone. "Oh, it's later than I thought. I dropped off the kids a while ago, but Jay and I got talking. I didn't realize how long I'd been here, actually. I should get going."

Adrian glanced between them. "You certainly don't have to leave on my account," he said, amused. He sat down beside Jay and kissed his cheek. "Don't get me wrong. I'm grateful, but could someone explain what's going on here?"

Michelle laughed. "What's going on is that your boyfriend is quite charming, and we discovered we have a common interest."

"Other than the children?" Adrian asked.

"Yes. Stained glass windows," Jay said.

Adrian gaped at him. "Wait, what? Can we rewind this conversation?" Adrian asked. "I think I missed something. Or maybe a lot of somethings."

Michelle laughed again. "Let me see if I can catch you up. I dropped the kids off earlier, and while Jay and I were chatting for a few minutes, Josh decided to color. Do you remember those coloring book sheets I printed off for the kids?"

"Yeah, vaguely."

"Well, there are a couple that are of stained-glass windows. Jay and I got to talking about the fact that we both like stained glass and thought it would be interesting to learn how to make it."

"Okay," Adrian said, still a little bewildered by the whole thing.

"So we're talking about taking a class together," Michelle said, beaming.

"There are stained glass making classes?" Adrian asked. It wasn't really the thing he wanted to ask, but he wasn't even sure where to begin with any of the other questions he had.

"Sure," Michelle said. "There's a place about twenty minutes from here, actually."

"Okay, good to know," Adrian said faintly.

"So we were thinking of going. They offer classes one Saturday morning a month, and I think it'll be fun."

Adrian looked between his boyfriend and his ex-wife. "You're really going together?"

A concerned expression crossed Jay's face. "Do you have a problem with that? I know you're usually at the bakery on Saturday mornings, but I'm sure between the three of us we can work out childcare. Your mom has been bugging us to give her more time with the kids, so I thought maybe we could ask her. I hope I didn't overstep, though …"

"No, no," Adrian protested. "It's perfectly fine. My mom will be thrilled, and I think it's great if you two want to hang out. I just didn't expect it."

"You should see your face right now, Adrian," Michelle said, giggling. "I've never seen you look so confused."

Adrian shook his head, trying to clear it. He felt a bit like he'd stepped into some sort of alternate dimension. "No, this is great. I think it's fantastic you two get along so well. It can only be good for the kids, but stained glass classes? I did not see that coming."

Michelle left a short while later, giggling again as she promised to text Jay about registering for the class.

A desperate need to do laundry and get caught up on a few things around the house put all thoughts about Adrian's ex-wife from his mind, but a few hours later, thoughts of Michelle resurfaced.

"Hey, I almost forgot. I have a question for you," Adrian said as he matched up a small pair of striped socks.

Jay looked up from the kids' T-shirts he'd been folding. "What's that?"

"I had an email from Seth asking how we felt about Michelle and Shane coming to the wedding. You good with that?"

"It's fine by me," Jay said with a little shrug. "Unless it's weird for you."

"No, I'm good with her being there." Adrian grinned. "Besides, she can help keep an eye on the kids if we need it."

Jay chuckled. "Your whole family is going to be there. Those kids have more people to take care of them than most."

"Oh, I know," Adrian said. "We're very lucky. So, I can let Seth know we're good with Michelle coming?"

"Absolutely," Jay said firmly. "Michelle is always going to be a big part of your life because of the kids, and if I have anything to say about it, I'm going to be here too."

"You better be!"

Jay smiled as he stood. "Besides, I like Michelle."

"Apparently." Adrian snorted. He set the stacks of folded clothes into the laundry basket to carry upstairs later. "I still can't believe my ex-wife and my new boyfriend are going to be learning how to make stained glass windows together but …"

"I can honestly say I never expected it either, but it seemed like a fun idea. You sure you're okay with it?"

"Yeah, of course." Adrian stood, then wrapped his arms around Jay and pulled him closer. "Honestly, it's fantastic. But I thought Michelle had a problem with me being bi. So if that weekend we met, if you would have told me a year-and-a-half later, you and my ex-wife would be taking art classes together, I would have keeled over from a heart attack."

Jay patted his chest. "No heart attacks, baby. I want you around to love for as long as possible."

"To love?" Adrian held his breath. They hadn't spoken that word to each other yet. Adrian had felt it for a while though. The feeling had hit him sometime during their first trip to the zoo with the kids. Jay had put Josh on his shoulders so he could get a better look at the giraffes while he listened intently to the animal facts Molly was reading aloud from the sign. Adrian had taken one look at that and fallen head over heels. For good. There was no turning back.

But he'd wondered if it was too soon to declare his feelings. At that point, he and Jay had only been dating for about a month and a half, and he hadn't wanted to push him. It was more than enough that Jay was taking an active role in the kids' lives and seemed to be enjoying it. Seemed to be thriving in the role, actually.

"You haven't figured out by now that I love you?" Jay asked. He smoothed Adrian's hair behind his ears.

"You've shown me you have," Adrian said. "But you haven't said the words aloud, and I didn't want to rush you."

"I thought *I* might be rushing *you*."

"Nope." Adrian stole a kiss. "I've loved you since the giraffes."

A puzzled frown crossed Jay's face. "Since the giraffes?"

Adrian laughed. "I'll tell you what I mean later. Right now, I need to kiss you."

"Mmm, I'm okay with that." Jay leaned in and kissed Adrian.

He closed his eyes as he threaded a hand through Jay's hair, teasing the seam of his mouth with his tongue. Jay opened to him just as something slammed up against his leg. "What're we having for dinner?"

Adrian stifled a groan, then pulled away from Jay to look down at his son. "Well, I'm not sure, actually." He usually tried to plan ahead, but it had been a very busy week. "How would you feel about Chinese takeout?"

"Yesss," Josh said. "I want two egg rolls!"

"We will order two for you, but you have to eat some other food too. Like … maybe some chicken and broccoli. Think you could manage that?"

Josh cheered. "I'm gonna eat all the broccoli!"

"Okay, weirdo," Adrian said as he gently pushed him toward the stairs. "You can have all the broccoli. But first, you need to go ask your sister what she wants."

After Josh had gone thundering up the wooden steps, Adrian turned to look at Jay, who was staring at him with a look of wonder on his face. Adrian gave him a puzzled smile. "What's that look for?"

"Holy shit. I trust you. I don't just love you. I *trust* you. It just hit me all of a sudden that I completely trust that you won't give up on us." Jay swallowed hard. "I trust that you're in this for the long haul."

"I am so in this," Adrian said as he wove their fingers together, slightly stunned by Jay's declaration. "Every step of the way, as long as you're by my side."

Jay pulled him in for another searing kiss.

Which, of course, got interrupted by the kids because that seemed to be their favorite pastime. But later that night, as the four of them ate Chinese takeout around the dining room table, Adrian thought how lucky he was. He had to pinch himself to be sure it was real.

He had a great relationship with Jay and with his ex-wife. The kids were totally on board with Jay being in their lives. There was just one more hurdle they needed to overcome.

Winning over the Sunagars.

August 2019 – Pittsburgh, Pennsylvania

Gaish and Maaheshvari Sunagar had been unhappy about the idea of Jay's move to Pittsburgh, and Adrian's presence in his life hadn't helped the situation. The first, brief meeting between Adrian and the Sunagars in New York had been tense, and

Adrian hadn't felt particularly welcome. But they'd recently accepted Jay invitation to visit Pittsburgh to have dinner at Adrian's place, so Adrian was hopeful they'd get there eventually.

He wondered if his stomach would ever recover from the nerves, but he was hopeful.

"Okay." Adrian squatted down to meet Molly and Josh at eye-level. "You remember what we talked about for meeting Jay's parents?"

Molly nodded. "Their culture is a little different than ours, but we should be respectful," she parroted back. Adrian smiled, hearing his words come out of her mouth.

"Exactly." He hesitated. He'd debated if he should say anything about the fact that Jay and his parents didn't get along with each other the way Adrian got along with his family. But the one thing he didn't want to do was set them all up for failure by warning the kids of that and having that taint their impression of the Sunagars. No, best to wait and see how it went. If it got ugly, Adrian would send the kids upstairs.

At the sound of a knock on the door, Adrian's heart leaped in his throat. He opened it to see Jay and his parents.

"Please, come in." Adrian smiled at them. "It's good to see you again, Mr. and Mrs. Sunagar."

"Gaish and Maaheshvari is fine," Jay's father said.

Adrian held his hand out to Gaish. His hair had gone almost completely silver, and the first time Adrian met him, he'd wondered if Jay's hair would turn that color eventually. It would be a very handsome look on him.

Maaheshvari's hair was still black, but he assumed she dyed it. Her gaze was assessing as she shook Adrian's hand. "You really do look so much like your brother."

Adrian smiled at her. "We've been told that before. Our brother Mitchell also has similar features and coloring. Thankfully, Seth's twin sister Sarah got all of the pretty genes in the family."

Maaheshvari gave him a faint smile. "I hope Seth and Erik are well."

"They are. Very busy right now with wedding planning, though." Adrian had considered having Seth and Erik over to help ease the tension, but he figured if he couldn't win over the Sunagars on his own, he was in trouble long-term. And these days, between the wedding and Seth's travel, it was difficult for him to make it to Pittsburgh.

"Is your other brother also gay?" Maaheshvari asked.

"No, he's married to a woman, and they have a couple kids." Adrian belatedly remembered he hadn't introduced his own kids yet. *Shit.* He glanced over at them, amazed they'd been standing there so quietly. "These are my kids, Molly and Josh. Please say hi to Jay's parents."

The kids shyly said hello, then tucked themselves behind Adrian. Which was odd because Molly generally wasn't shy about anything. But maybe Adrian's nerves had worn off on her. A glance over at Jay wasn't reassuring either. He looked very quiet and very nervous. Right, okay, so Adrian was on his own.

Maaheshvari held out a small container to him. "I couldn't bring much on the plane, but I made some *mithai*—sweets—for you. Coconut *ladoo* are Jay's favorite and I thought you might like to try them." Her smile seemed tentative.

"That was so thoughtful," Adrian said. "Thank you. I'm sure we'll all enjoy them. And please, come in the living room," Adrian said. "Can I get you anything to drink? I have coffee, tea, lemonade, sparkling water …" He knew better than to offer them alcohol.

They asked for tea, and Adrian carried the container of *ladoo* into the kitchen. He stared at it thoughtfully as the water boiled.

Jay had told him it was unthinkable for Desis to arrive empty handed, so Adrian had expected something—flowers or store-bought sweets perhaps—but they'd brought homemade treats, and Jay's favorite at that. It seemed like the Sunagars were making a real effort. It occurred to Adrian then that perhaps what seemed like reserve or coldness was actually nerves.

Maybe they were as nervous about this meeting as Adrian was. Whether or not the Sunagars approved of every choice Jay made, it was clear they loved him. And they'd flown all the way from New York to meet Adrian and the kids. That had to mean something. Perhaps they were worried that if they didn't make an effort, they would lose their son completely.

Adrian felt a sudden wave of sympathy for them. It must be very difficult in their position. They were trying, so he'd give them the benefit of the doubt.

The whistle of the kettle made him jerk in surprise, and he hastily turned off the burner and prepared the tea. He got lemonade for the kids, then carried a large tray into the living room.

The room seemed suspiciously quiet when he arrived, so when they were all seated with beverages, Adrian cleared his throat, hoping he could jumpstart the conversation. "Gaish, Maaheshvari, did you know Jay and I will be making Seth and Erik's wedding cake?"

"You're a pastry chef too, yes?" Gaish asked. It had come up the previous time they met, but Adrian wasn't too surprised he hadn't remembered. Adrian glanced over at Jay again. He still looked tense.

"Not exactly." Adrian cleared his throat. "I bake pastries, cakes, and bread, but my training was a little different. I do have a certification as a master baker." He enunciated carefully. "And I own my own bakery. We've been up and running for about six years."

A pleased expression crossed Gaish's face. "A business owner. Good." He sounded approving.

"It's challenging but very rewarding. After six years, we're turning a good profit, and I've hired a few new people lately. Seth helped me with some marketing that really allowed the business to grow."

"That's excellent."

They all went silent, and Adrian wracked his brain for another topic of conversation.

"I like your dress," Molly blurted out. She was seated on the floor not far from Maaheshvari, and she had been very quiet. Uncharacteristically so.

Maaheshvari looked down at her and smoothed her hand over the flowing fabric. It was a deep blue with a purple edge. Gaish wore trousers and a crisp blue button-down shirt. Adrian, Jay, and the kids had all dressed up as well. Perhaps they'd all been trying to impress each other. "It's not a dress. It's called a saree." Her tone was kind, though.

"Oh. I'm sorry. I didn't know. It's pretty. I like it."

Maaheshvari smiled. "What do you like about it?"

"The colors! And it looks soft." Molly held her hand out as if to touch it, but she hesitated, looking up at Maaheshvari as if asking for permission.

To Adrian's surprise, she held the hem of it out to Molly.

Molly's eyes lit up, and she carefully stroked it. "Ooh, it is soft."

"I have a lot of these at home in all sorts of colors. I buy them whenever I go home to India to visit. They come in every color of the rainbow, and some of them are much fancier than this one."

"Purple's my favorite," Molly said. "And sometimes blue."

"Did you know Karnataka is the silk hub of India?" Gaish said proudly. "My family still exports it."

"That must be very interesting," Adrian said. "What made you decide to go into dentistry rather than the family business?"

"It's stable," Gaish said firmly. "While business was good for my family, my parents wanted more for me. They saw many families in Bangalore where bad marriages led to crushed dreams of a stable life. Many sacrificed for the well-being of their younger siblings. Maaheshvari was a good match, and being a dentist let me take care of my family. I've been able to help bring several of my nephews here to America as well."

Adrian nodded. Jay's parents' objections to his career and being gay made sense in that context. Adrian just had to show them that Jay's job and relationship were stable. Adrian wanted to prove to them he could be a good match for Jay too.

"Did Jay tell you how well his new job is going?" Adrian prompted. He knew Jay wouldn't bring it up himself.

"Yeah, I got a raise last month," Jay said quietly. "And because the cost of living is so much better here, I'm able to put more into savings."

Gaish nodded approvingly. "Good. Good."

Adrian wasn't going to bring up the fact that he and Jay were talking about moving in together soon. Jay's six-month lease would be up in September, and Adrian had discussed it with the kids. They were all for Jay moving in, but Adrian wasn't sure how that would go over with Jay's parents.

Adrian glanced at the time on the clock. He needed to get started on the second part of dinner soon if they were going to eat at reasonable time tonight.

"Maaheshvari?" Adrian said. "I was wondering if you could give me your opinion. Seth gave me the recipe for your *bisi bele bhath* and I would love your feedback on it to make sure I got it right."

She looked surprised, but she nodded. "If you'd like."

"Please, it would be helpful." *Dear God, I want to impress you,* Adrian thought wildly. *Let me get this right.*

She followed Adrian into the kitchen, and he lifted the lid on the pot that had been simmering all afternoon. It was a rice and lentil dish with vegetables and at least a dozen spices. Hopefully, he hadn't screwed it up. He handed her a spoon.

Maaheshvari tasted the dish carefully. "Close. A bit more fenugreek."

She inspected his spices, then handed the bottle of the seeds to Adrian. "These are good quality." She sounded a little surprised as she sniffed a bottle of coriander seeds.

"Jay and I have been shopping at an Indian market here in Pitts-burgh." Adrian put a pinch of the fenugreek seeds into a mortar and pestle, then ground them between the pieces of stone.

"You grind them yourself." She sounded *very* surprised at that.

He smiled at her. "Yes. I knew they'd be fresher that way, and I wanted to get this right."

"I use a coffee grinder. Much easier."

Adrian laughed. "That would be easier."

"Get one just for your spices," she said. "You don't want jeera in your coffee."

"I don't," Adrian agreed with a little laugh. "Though cardamom is nice."

"You should toast your spices in a dry pan first too. It brings out the flavor."

Adrian groaned. "I did that earlier, but I forgot just now." Damn it, he'd been hoping to impress her.

"You'll learn." The corner of her mouth turned up.

"I know. I just wanted this to be perfect," he admitted. "I was very nervous about tonight going well."

Her expression grew soft. "You love my son."

"Yes," Adrian agreed. "Very much."

"And you make him happy."

"I'm certainly trying."

"Your kids love him too."

"They do."

She nodded as if he'd passed some sort of test, then turned her attention back to the food as he sprinkled the fenugreek in the lentil dish. "That's enough," she warned him.

He set the mortar and pestle with the remaining powder aside, and she nodded at the bowl covered in plastic wrap on the counter.

"You're making dosa."

"Yes." He'd made three batches of the savory crepe-like pancakes in the past week, hoping to master the technique. "I'm going to try, anyway. I can't seem to get it quite right. They're either too thin or too thick."

"Let me wash my hands and I'll show you the right way to make them."

"I'd like that very much," he said, not even trying to hide his relief. They were definitely making progress.

When they all settled down at the dinner table half an hour later, Gaish looked surprised when Adrian ladled some of the *bisi bele bhath* onto the kids' plates. "Your children will eat that?"

"They'll try it," Adrian said. "They're expected to try everything on their plate at least once. But they have pretty adventurous palates."

"I love broccoli and most vegetables, and people tell me I'm weird!" Josh piped up and everyone chuckled. Even Jay's parents looked amused. Jay still looked tense, though, and Adrian nudged Jay's foot with his own.

Jay's gaze flicked up to him, and he managed a small smile. *We've got this*, Adrian tried to convey with his gaze. Jay nodded as if he'd gotten the message.

Everyone tucked into their food, and Adrian was relieved when Maaheshvari gave him an approving little nod. "Very good."

"This is good," Gaish said. He sounded quite surprised, but Adrian couldn't really blame him.

"Well, it's Maaheshvari's recipe," Adrian said charitably. "And she cooked most of the dosa."

"They *are* good," Jay said, picking one up. He was beginning to look a little more relaxed.

"What do you think, kids?" Adrian asked. He turned to look at Josh's plate, only to find all of the dosa and at least half of the lentil dish gone. "I'm guessing you liked it," he said drily.

Josh nodded emphatically, cramming more lentils into his mouth with his fork. Okay, maybe they needed to work on table manners still but ...

"A good appetite is good for a growing boy," Maaheshvari said approvingly. "Ajay was picky. He wanted American food. He didn't like what I made."

Jay gestured toward his plate. "I like both now."

"It's good you have Adrian to cook Indian dishes for you." Maaheshvari looked over at Adrian. "I'll send you some more of my recipes."

"That would be great," Adrian said, genuinely pleased by the gesture.

"Adrian was very nervous, you know," Jay said. "That you might not like him. He worked very hard to impress you."

Adrian ducked his head. "I did. I know this is isn't easy for you, but I wanted you to see that I could be good for your son."

"We were nervous too," Gaish said. "We didn't know how you'd feel about us."

Once they had all that out in the open, the rest of the dinner passed quite pleasantly. Adrian's apprehension faded, and the conversation flowed better as they moved on to other things. It turned out Gaish watched American football, so they discussed draft picks and the upcoming season, and Adrian felt a wave of relief as the remaining tension left him. Finally, some common ground.

After dinner, Jay put on his shoes to run his parents back to the hotel where they were staying. He'd been learning to drive after spending most of his life as a non-driving New Yorker and had passed his driver's test recently. Adrian was so proud of him.

"We'll go to the zoo tomorrow, then," Adrian suggested when they all stood by the door.

Maaheshvari smiled at him. "Yes. That would be very nice."

"We'll pick you up at ten, if that's all right?" Adrian said.

They nodded and said their goodbyes before Jay gently herded them out the door. The kids disappeared into the living room to play while Adrian put away the leftovers and loaded the dishwasher. He'd nearly finished cleaning up when Jay walked into the kitchen.

He looked exhausted. Adrian knew the feeling.

"I think that went pretty well," Adrian said. He dried his hands and walked over to stand by Jay. Jay sagged against him, and Adrian wrapped his arms around his boyfriend.

"I think that went *very* well," Jay said. "I mean, we're probably always going to be at odds in some ways, but they like you. They like the kids. And they didn't make a single comment about me moving back to New York so …"

"Sounds like a win to me." Adrian kissed his temple.

"Thank you for everything you did," Jay said seriously. "I know this was stressful, and you put a lot of work into making my mom's recipe and …"

Adrian shrugged. "I know food. It seemed like as good a way as any to connect with them. And I remembered what you said about your ex."

Jay chuckled. "Well, it worked. The kids were a big help too. I think the idea of having grandkids was a selling point to my parents. They thought they'd never get them from me."

"Grandkids," Adrian said with a smile. "You're planning to stick around for a while then, huh?"

"If you and the kids will have me."

Adrian closed his eyes and leaned his forehead against Jay's. "Definitely."

"Then I'm not going anywhere."

"Perfect." Adrian snuck a kiss. "Now, how about you help me get the kids to bed?"

"I can do that."

"Time for bed," Adrian called out. "Josh, Molly, go up and brush your teeth."

There was a little whining, but eventually, they did as they were told.

"You want me to read you a story?" Adrian asked a short while later, leaning against the doorframe into Josh's room.

"No. I want Jay to."

"Well, okay, then," Adrian said with a laugh. He walked in and kissed Josh's forehead.

"Out of the way," Jay said with a little wink as Adrian turned to leave. "You're not wanted here."

"I can see where I stand in this family," Adrian said. He reached out and squeezed Jay's hand. He squeezed back.

"Okay, what do you want me to read tonight?" Jay asked as he took a seat on the edge of Josh's bed.

"The one about the dump truck!"

"I can do that." Jay took the book from Josh's outstretched hand.

Adrian leaned in the doorway for a moment as he watched Jay read aloud. It brought a lump to Adrian's throat. This, right here, was everything he'd ever wanted. A cozy house, a thriving bakery, two happy kids, and a partner who loved him. He was a lucky, lucky man.

———

"I think I'm developing a fetish for that look."

Adrian glanced up from his phone, peering at Jay over the rim of his glasses. "Which one?"

"The hot boyfriend with glasses one."

Adrian chuckled as he set his phone aside. "My eyes were tired so I took out my contacts."

"Trust me, I wasn't complaining." Jay dropped onto the couch beside Adrian. "I read two stories to Josh tonight."

"Pushover," Adrian teased.

"I can't resist the pout," Jay said with a little sigh. "He gets it from you, you know?"

"He does not," Adrian protested. "Take that back."

"You're doing it right now!"

"I am?"

"You *so* are," Jay said drily.

"Hmm. Does that mean it'll get me what I want?"

"I don't know. What *do* you want?"

Adrian grabbed the front of Jay's shirt. "You." He pulled him in for a searing, dirty kiss.

"Thought we were going to watch that movie tonight," Jay said when he drew back. His lips were shiny and pink from Adrian's kiss.

Adrian glanced over at the screen. "You're choosing a moving instead of taking your man to bed?"

Jay hummed. "Well, when you put it like that …"

"That's what I thought." Adrian clicked off the TV and stood.

"Shower first?"

"Sounds good." Adrian strode out of the living room. "Let's make it quick, though. Your ass is mine tonight."

The sound of Jay's quiet laughter followed Adrian as he jogged up the stairs, and a few moments later, so did Jay.

———

"Why are you teasing me like this?" Jay whined half an hour later as he lay sprawled out on Adrian's bed.

Adrian flicked his tongue against Jay's nipple. "Like what?"

"Like *this*. I need you, Adrian."

He drew his teeth across the sensitive peak before sucking gently. Jay's hips bowed up—or would have if Adrian hadn't been planted firmly between his thighs, pressing him down into the mattress—so Adrian did it again.

"You have me."

Jay let out an aggravated huff. "Not what I meant."

"Maybe you should explain it." Adrian slid a little lower, working his way down Jay's chest and stomach with more teasing little flicks of his tongue.

"Need you to fuck me."

"I will."

"Now," Jay growled.

"Nope." Adrian dragged his tongue along Jay's hipbone. "I'm going to take my time. You've been too tense this week for me to do this."

"I'm tense now," Jay grumbled. "Because you aren't fucking me."

Adrian pressed his face against Jay's lower abdomen to stifle his laughter, but it didn't work very well, and a snort escaped him. When he lifted his head, Jay was looking at him with a fond expression. "I just ruined the mood, didn't I?"

"No." Adrian smiled back. "Never."

"Thank goodness."

Adrian slid back up Jay's body and pinned him to the bed, his elbows beside Jay's ears. "God, I love you."

"I love you too." Jay slid his hands up and down Adrian's back. "If I didn't say it already, thank you for everything you did tonight. I know I kinda froze up on you."

"Hey, it's okay." Adrian smoothed Jay's hair back. "You've done a lot for me in the past six months. You uprooted your whole life to take a gamble on moving to Pittsburgh to be with me. You helped me keep my business running. You welcomed my kids wholeheartedly into your life. The least I can do is make an attempt to show your parents that I'm good for you."

"You are," Jay said. "You have made me so happy. And I can't wait to move in with you."

"I can't wait either. I already made space in the closet for you, in fact," Adrian said with a smile. "It's going to be so nice having you here permanently. I hate it when I have to sleep alone."

"I'm here most nights." Jay's smile seemed to stretch from cheek to cheek, and his brown eyes were warm and happy.

"But I want you *every* night," Adrian countered. He leaned in and kissed Jay again.

Jay let out a quiet sound of pleasure before burying his hand in Adrian's hair and deepening it. Adrian's heart felt very full as he tried to pour every bit of feeling he had for Jay into the kiss. He reluctantly pulled back but only to kiss his way down Jay's body again. This time, Jay didn't push Adrian to move any faster.

When Adrian slid his mouth down over Jay's cock, Jay threaded his fingers through Adrian's hair and held on tight. Sweet, slow strokes brought Jay to a point where he was shaking, and then Adrian sat back, reaching for the lube. The soft gasps Jay made when Adrian worked him open with his fingers were music to Adrian's ears, but the low groan he made when Adrian slid his cock inside was even better.

But when Adrian pushed deeper, he drew a strangled gasp from Jay's lips. "Fuck, Adrian!"

"Shh." Adrian pressed his lips against Jay's. "Quiet." They kissed as Adrian reveled in the tight, slick feel of Jay's body surrounding his cock. Whether he was inside Jay or Jay was inside him, it was always so good.

Kisses became panting breaths against each other's lips as Jay used his hands to urge Adrian to move faster. And when Jay cried out in orgasm, Adrian muffled the sound with his lips and kissed him again.

EPILOGUE

Unmitigated chaos was the best way to describe the scene in front of Adrian. The Cobb family along with the rest of Seth and Erik's families and friends had taken over the Williamsville Inn, and it was complete and utter madness. As best man, Adrian should probably be doing something to organize it, but there was supposed to be a wedding planner around here somewhere, and wasn't that her job?

A moment later, Adrian spotted her as she barked orders at a roadie. Which was a super weird thing to see at a wedding, but that's what happened when someone like Rex Garland was singing at it. Adrian still couldn't get over it. As crazy and improbable as it seemed, Rex, Will, Seth, and Erik had become fast friends. Who'd have thought a celebrity that big would see Seth's posts about the inn, meet the love of his life there, and send him a private message? While the plan had started out as a cordial offer to perform and do double-duty as the kick-off to the social media marketing campaign for the inn's newly revamped event space, it was clearly deeper than that now.

Rex had made a touching speech at the rehearsal dinner last night, and Adrian had felt a little star-struck when he introduced himself.

Of course, someone of Rex's fame couldn't just perform without an entourage of people to help set up the equipment and secure the building to keep fans from storming the wedding. So what might have been a quiet, intimate wedding had become something much, much larger.

It was going to be amazing, but Adrian vowed that when and Jay tied the knot, they'd do it in a much more sedate fashion. Then he remembered that his boyfriend's family would probably never allow that. They might be able to manage a small courthouse ceremony for the actual wedding, but there would probably be a large Hindu ceremony as well. The thought made Adrian feel a little overwhelmed, but as he glanced over to see Jay helping Josh straighten his bow tie, he felt a smile creep over his face.

In the past six months, their relationship had moved steadily toward where they were now. The kids adored Jay, and they'd found a good routine now that he was living with them.

A fantastic personal life wasn't the only thing Adrian had to feel good about either. King of Tarts was thriving. After six months, Adrian was cautiously optimistic that the Valentine's Day cupcake promotion hadn't been a flash-in-the-pan moment of success. Thankfully, regular business wasn't quite as intense as it had been on Valentine's Day, but there was no question that sales were up at least forty percent over the previous year. Adrian was overjoyed. He'd rolled some of the profits back into the business by making a few badly needed updates to the kitchen and hiring a professional food photographer to update the photos on his website.

He'd also given his previous employees raises and hired two new full-time people along with two more who were seasonal help. It was enough that he'd been able to take time off for Seth's wedding and plan a vacation with Jay and the kids for a couple of weeks after.

Jay's position as head pastry chef at a restaurant was going exceptionally well too. The executive chef there was enthusiastic about his work, and when Jay had broached the idea of using a few traditional Indian *mithai* recipes as flavor inspiration for some of his desserts, she'd embraced the idea, and the dishes had proved to be very popular.

Maaheshvari had emailed Adrian some family recipes, which had opened up a line of communication between them. Adrian occasionally sent her questions about cooking techniques and attached numerous photos of the kids. Adrian had yet to meet Jay's sisters but he'd be doing that in a couple of weeks, and while things weren't perfect between Jay and his parents, now that they knew Jay was settling down and his career was thriving once again, they were all a lot happier.

Now, Adrian and Jay stood in the middle of the courtyard as people scurried around them getting things prepped for the wedding. The cake had been baked, assembled, and decorated over the past few days, and it was now waiting inside in the room where the food was set up for the reception. It was much too hot in the courtyard for the tiered Swiss meringue buttercream frosted cake, but the air conditioning of the hotel would keep it looking perfect until the grooms cut into it. They'd also made a variety of cupcakes and tortes as well, and Adrian had really enjoyed working with Jay on the project. While there were probably more desserts than the guests could eat tonight, there were small boxes for everyone to take home as a favor.

"Adrian?" Jay prompted. "You okay? What's got you thinking so hard?"

"Oh, sorry. Just thinking about how far we've come. How did I get so damn lucky?" Adrian murmured with a smile, tightening his grip around Jay. He looked very handsome in a gray suit with a peacock blue button-down.

"I don't know. But I think somebody should probably bottle the water from the hotels in New York because, at this rate, they'll make millions off its matchmaking capabilities."

Adrian laughed. "So you think that's the cause of all this pairing up?"

"I don't know, but it worked for Seth and Eric." Jay nodded toward the happy couple. "Plus Rex and Will. Certainly worked for us too."

"Certainly did," Adrian agreed.

Adrian had spent a lot of time in the past few years wondering where his marriage had gone wrong. He could list a few things: getting together too young, not being able to grow and change together, a lack of communication. They were all true. And he was mindful of the latter two with Jay.

But now he felt like maybe life had led him exactly where he needed to be. Michelle was happy with Shane. Adrian was deliriously happy with Jay. Together, he and Michelle had made two beautiful kids, and now they were co-parenting them, albeit in a far different way than either of them had originally anticipated. And with a little extra help these days.

"Did Michelle really give Seth and Erik a piece of stained-glass art for their wedding gift?"

"She did," Jay said with a smile. "Turns out she's really damn good at it."

Adrian snorted. "It still makes me laugh to think about you two taking classes together. You're both so weird."

"You love us."

"I do," Adrian agreed. And frankly, he was damn grateful Jay and Michelle got along so well. With as busy as they all were, it made shuffling kids around so much easier when they were all comfortable with Jay taking a big role in that. He leaned in. "But there's only one of you whose clothes I want to rip off after this wedding."

"It better be me." Jay grinned widely. "Or we're going to have to have a conversation."

"It is most definitely you," Adrian assured him. "In fact, there is a tub of frosting in the refrigerator in our room as we speak."

"Oh, is there?"

"There is," Adrian said. "And I think as long as we remember to lock the connecting door to the kids' room tonight ..."

Jay laughed. They'd nearly gotten caught with their pants down last night when Josh had come in because he'd spotted a bee in his room. It had been a very stressful few moments while Adrian had faked a sense of calm as he asked Josh to go back to his room and close the door. Adrian assured him he'd be there in just a minute, as he desperately hoped his son didn't drag him naked from the bed to vanquish the stinging beast. Jay looked even more horrified than Adrian had felt, and after they'd both put on pants, Adrian had needed to reassure him it wouldn't have been the end of the world even if they did accidentally flash the kid. It was all part of being a parent. Life very rarely went according to plan.

"Yeah, no more repeats of last night," Jay agreed. "We check the door three times before the pants come off."

"Deal."

"Adrian, we need to get some pictures of the wedding party now," the wedding planner said. "Can you go over by the white rose arch?"

"Oh. Sure, one sec." Adrian let go of Jay with a quick kiss to the temple. "Guess it's time for me to do my job. I'll see you after the ceremony?"

"Yes," Jay said. "You better save me a dance too."

"You get all the dances," Adrian said.

Jay laugh. "I'm quite sure Molly will have something to say about that. Not to mention your mom and sister."

"Oh, good point," Adrian said. "Well, you'll get most of them. Love you."

Jay's smile was brilliant. "I love you too."

———

Several hours later, Adrian wrapped his arms around Jay and rested their temples together as they swayed to Rex Garland's voice. The ceremony had gone off without a hitch, the dinner and cake cutting had been perfect, and Adrian had even made the crowd laugh with his best man speech. As happy as Adrian was for the grooms, he was looking forward to no longer thinking about them and enjoying the rest of the evening with the man he loved.

"Are you happy?" Adrian asked quietly.

Jay sighed contently and tightened his grip on Adrian's torso. "Never been happier."

"Me neither." Adrian licked his lips. In fact, there was a ring box tucked in his luggage that he desperately hoped Jay wouldn't stumble across. They were going to visit Niagara Falls next week with the kids, and if everything went according to plan, he'd ask Jay to marry him there.

They'd had to work hard at this. Burying old hurts. Building trust between them again. That had all taken time and patience. Thank God, Jay had meshed seamlessly with the Cobb family because it hadn't been easy navigating Jay's relationship with his parents and introducing Adrian and the kids to them. But it had all been worth it.

"I have an idea," Adrian blurted out. Fuck his plan. He suddenly couldn't wait another second to ask Jay.

"Yeah? What's that?" Jay gave him a puzzled smile.

"I think we should get married next year. On Valentine's Day."

Jay stilled, then drew back to look Adrian in the eye. "Are you proposing to me?"

"I mean, not officially. I was going to propose at the falls, and I don't want to take away from Seth and Erik's big day. But if you say yes, we can announce it after they get back from their honeymoon in Tahiti."

"And if I don't say yes?"

Adrian didn't even flinch. "We'll talk about it and figure out what works for both of us."

A slow smile bloomed across Jay's face. "The answer is yes."

"Oh, thank God," Adrian said. He leaned in and kissed Jay. "Because I very much want to spend the rest of my life with you, Ajay Sunagar."

"I want that too. You and the kids," Jay said. "Why Valentine's Day, though? Isn't that one of your biggest sales days at the bakery?"

"It is," Adrian said. "But I trust Henry to handle it, if need be. It doesn't have to be on Valentine's Day, anyway, but I kind of think of that as our anniversary."

"Not a year and a half ago in January when we met in New York for the first time? Or this past February when we met again?"

"No," Adrian said thoughtfully. "That was a botched trial."

Jay laughed. "Like when you try a new cake recipe that flops."

"Exactly. It doesn't count." Adrian smiled at Jay as they continued to sway to the music. "Valentine's Day is when it all came together."

The End

If you loved Adrian and Jay's romantic Valentine's Day story, check out *Date in a Pinch*.

When chemistry teacher Neil gets an unexpected delivery at the high school where he works, he's mortified when his crush, Alexander, sees the contents. Curious but inexperienced with kink, Neil has no idea how to live out his fantasies until the hot lit teacher offers a helping hand. Grab it now!

Pendleton Bay Books

Visit the fictional small town of Pendleton Bay on the shores of Lake Michigan. All books set in this universe can be read as standalones but characters from other books/series may appear from time to time.

There are three series set within the Pendleton Bay Universe.

Naughty in Pendleton Series

An ongoing m/m romance series set in the town of Pendleton Bay with characters exploring the kinkier side of romance. BDSM elements will appear in all books.

Date in a Pinch: When chemistry teacher Neil gets an unexpected delivery at the high school where he works, he's mortified when his crush, Alexander, sees the contents. Curious but inexperienced with kink, Neil has no idea how to live out his fantasies until the hot lit teacher offers a helping hand

Safety in Numbers**:** Coming 2021

Flirty in Pendleton Series

An ongoing m/m romance series set in the town of Pendleton Bay.

Geeks, Nerds, and Cuddles**:** Re-release 2021

Doc Brodie and the Big, Purple Cat Toy**:** Re-release 2021

Poly in Pendleton Series

An ongoing m/m/f romance series set in the town of Pendleton Bay.

Three Shots: Re-release February 26, 2021

Between the Studs: Re-release 2021

———

Peachtree Books

Visit the real life city of Atlanta, Georgia. All books in this universe can be read as standalone but characters from both series do crossover.

There are two series set with the Peachtree Universe.

The Peachtree Series

Complete, continuous m/m series featuring an age gap, light kink, and found family

Off-Balance: Coworkers Russ & Stephen meet over a spilled cup of coffee and navigate the complexities of a nineteen-year age gap, a big difference in income, and the death of Stephen's estranged father.

Love in the Balance: Their story continues as Russ introduces Stephen to his family, searches for his absent mother, and asks Stephen to marry him.

Full Balance: They navigate new challenges as they take in a teenage foster boy named Austin and decide to make him a permanent part of their family.

Peachtree Place

Standalone m/m books in the same universe as The Peachtree Series

Trust the Connection: Evan & Jeremy find a love that will heal both their scars in this slow-burn, age-gap romance about living with a disability, believing in yourself, and building the family you always wanted.

———

The Midwest Series

Complete m/m series featuring four couples. Stories intertwine but can be read as standalones. Opposites attract m/m sports romance with numerous bisexual characters.

Bully & Exit: Drama geek Caleb is sure he'll never forgive Nathan, the hockey player who dumped him in high school, until he learns the real reason why in this slow-burn, second-chance new adult romance.

Push & Pull: Lowell & Brent have nothing in common when they leave on a summer road trip, but by the end, the makeup-wearing fashionista and the macho hockey player will realize they're perfect for each other in this enemies to lovers, slow-burn story about acceptance.

Touch & Go: Micah, a closeted pro pitcher, and Justin, a laid-back physical therapist, have nothing in common but when Micah blows out his shoulder, he'll have to choose which he wants more: baseball or love? An enemies to lovers, out for you romance.

Advance & Retreat: When fate brings Ian and Ricky together, a college swimmer will have to figure out how to reached for the gold without losing the sweet hotel manager who lights up the stage as sizzling drag queen Rosie Riveting. An age gap sports romance with a gender fluid character.

The West Hills

Standalone m/m series featuring three different couples

The Ghosts Between Us: Losing his brother in a devastating accident sends Chris spiraling into grief. The last person he expects to find comfort in is his brother's secret boyfriend, Elliot, in this slow burn, hurt/comfort romance.

Tidal Series – Co-authored with K Evan Coles

A complete, continuous m/m duology that takes Riley & Carter from best friends to lovers in this slow-burn romance featuring the sons of two wealthy Manhattan families.

Wake: After a decade and a half of lying to himself and everyone around him, Riley slowly come to terms with his sexuality and his feelings for his best friend, Carter, shattering their friendship.

Calm: Carter reaches his own realization and they slowly build the relationship they've been denying for so long.

Speakeasy Series – Co-authored with K Evan Coles

Complete, standalone m/m series featuring characters from the Tidal universe

With a Twist: After Will learns of his estranged father's cancer diagnosis, he returns home and slowly mends fences with him and falls in love with his father's colleague, David. Enemies to lovers, opposites attract, interracial romance.

Extra Dirty: Wealthy, pansexual businessman Jesse is perfectly happy living his life to the fullest with no strings attached, but when he meets Cam, a music teacher and DJ, he'll find that some strings are worth hanging onto in this age-gap, opposites-attract romance.

Behind the Stick: Speakeasy owner and bartender Kyle has taken a break from dating when he's rescued by Harlem fire-fighter Luka. Interracial romance and hurt/comfort.

Straight Up: When hot, tattooed biker chef Stuart meets quiet and serious Malcolm, they both have secrets they're hiding. Gray ace, bisexual awakening, lingerie kink.

The Williamsville Inn

Standalone m/m holiday romances in a shared universe with Hank Edwards

Snowstorms and Second Chances: Erik and Seth don't hit it off at first, but when a snowstorm leads to them sharing a room at a hotel, Erik discovers a whole new side of himself and his feelings about the holidays. A forced-proximity, bisexual-awakening romance with a second chance at happiness.

The Cupcake Conundrum: Adrian comes face to face with the biggest mistake of his past, Ajay, a hookup who he ghosted on. He'll have to make amends and win Jay's heart back in this single dad, second-chance interracial romance.

Colors Series

A continuous f/f series featuring a bisexual character and opposites attract trope

A Brighter Palette: When Annie, a struggling American freelance writer, meets Siobhán, a successful Irish painter living in Boston, the heat between them is undeniable, but is it enough to build something that will last?

The Greenest Isle: After Siobhán's father has a heart attack, she and Annie travel to Ireland to care for him. Their relationship is tested as they navigate living in a new place and healing old wounds.

Standalone Books

Baby, It's Cold Inside: Meeting Nate's parents doesn't go at all like Emerson planned. But there might be a Christmas miracle for the two of them before the visit is through in this sweet and funny m/m holiday romance.

Bromantic Getaway: Spencer is sure he's straight. But when an off-hand comment sends him tumbling into the realization he's in love with his best friend Devin, he'll have to turn a romantic vacation meant for his ex into the perfect opportunity to grab the love that's always been right in front of them in this best friends to lovers bi awakening m/m romance.

Cabin Fever: Kevin's best friend's dad is definitely off-limits. But he and Drew about to spend a week alone in a cabin the week before Christmas. And Kevin's never been any good at resisting temptation. An age gap, best friend's father m/m holiday romance.

Corked: A sommelier and a wine distributor clash in this enemies to lovers, age-gap m/m romance that takes Sean & Lucas from a restaurant in Chicago to owning a winery in Traverse City.

Inked in Blood: **Co-Authored with K Evan Coles** An unexpected event changes the life and death of a sexy, tattooed vampire named Jeff and Santiago, a tattoo artist with a secret. A paranormal, age-gap m/m romance.

Love in the Produce Aisle: Tyler's a disaster when it comes to cooking, but when Michael swoops in to rescue him, it's more than just the kitchen that's hot in this m/m opposites-attract short story.

Seeking Warmth: When Benny gets out of juvie, he's lost all hope for a future for him or his sister, but the help of his ex-boyfriend Scott will show him that hope and love still exist in this m/m YA novel about second chances.

The French Toast Emergencies: A series of grocery story mishaps leads to Arthur and Samuel sharing more than a loaf of bread during a sudden snowstorm in this forced-proximity m/m short story.

The Soldier Next Door: When Travis agrees to keep an eye on the guy next door for a few weeks while his parents are out of town, he never expects to fall in love with a soldier heading off to war. An age-gap m/m novella.

ABOUT THE AUTHOR

Brigham Vaughn is on the adventure of a lifetime as a full-time author. She devours books at an alarming rate and hasn't let her short arms and long torso stop her from doing yoga. She makes a killer key lime pie, hates green peppers, and loves wine tasting tours. A collector of vintage Nancy Drew books and green glassware, she enjoys poking around in antique shops and refinishing thrift store furniture. An avid photographer, she dreams of traveling the world and she can't wait to discover everything else life has to offer her.

Her books range from short stories to novellas to novels. They explore gay, bisexual, lesbian, and polyamorous romance in contemporary settings.

Want to read more of her work? Check it out on BookBub!

For news of new releases and sales, join her newsletter or follow on BookBub!

If you'd like to become an ARC reader, take part in giveaways, and get all of the latest news, please join her reader group, Brigham's Book Nerds. She'd love to have you there!